Books by J.P. Bowie

My Vampire and I

I0546100

My Vampire and I
My Vampire Lover
Duet in Blood
Blood Resurrection
Bound in Blood
Blood Lure
Blood Lust
Blood Talisman

Anthologies

Naughty Nooners
Saddle Up 'N Ride

Single Titles

Ride Em Cowboys Collection
Nowhere to Hide
Trip of a Lifetime
All I'll Ever Need
Evan Sent

Evan Sent

ISBN # 978-1-78686-162-7

Cover Art by Posh Gosh ©Copyright 2017

Interior text design by Claire Siemaszkiewicz

Pride Publishing

Published in 2017 by Pride Publishing, Think Tank, Ruston Way, Lincoln, LN6 7FL, United Kingdom.

Pride Publishing is a subsidiary of Totally Entwined Group Limited.

EVAN SENT

J.P. BOWIE

Dedication

My thanks, once again, to Claire and Nicki, the lovely ladies who run Pride Publishing, and to Sue Meadows, my editor who works so darned hard to make sure my stories appear seamless—and importantly, make sense! Thanks also to Susan and Kristin for pointing out the bloopers! Love to Phil, my hubby of 3 whole years on May 12th. After a long engagement of 22 years we finally made it.

Chapter One

Mark Henderson checked his voicemail for what had to be the twelfth time in the past two hours and let out a heavy sigh of disappointment and irritation. *Still nothing.*

"Damn." He was sure he would have heard *something* by now on his callback audition. The show's director had seemed to have been really pleased with Mark's reading, had raved about his headshots and full-body photographs then had asked a bunch of questions about him and his availability. He'd been almost certain it was a sure thing — and now this — not a word. The sinking feeling in the pit of his stomach grew into a nauseous ache at the thought of what it would mean if he didn't get the part.

Failure. Yep, not another word for it, and he could already hear the taunts of 'told ya so' from his friends and family, or what had passed for friends and family in Fairmont Hills, a conservative suburb of Spokane, Washington.

He almost dropped his phone from the shock of its strident chime. He'd turned the volume up so as not to miss that one important call. More disappointment.

"Hi, Kyle, what's up?"

"Well, don't sound so pleased to hear from me," Kyle snarked through his laughter.

"Sorry, I was expecting another call — the TV series I auditioned for last week? I had a callback this morning and they seemed really interested. They said they'd call me this afternoon..."

"It's only three o'clock, Mark. There's still time for them to call. Or maybe they just haven't come to a decision. You said there were at least a dozen guys there last week. It's pretty awesome you got the callback today. Don't give up on it yet."

Kyle's words of encouragement did little to comfort Mark. "I just have a feeling I'm not going to hear."

"Well, that would be shitty, if they don't call one way or the other."

"True, but it happens a lot, I'm afraid. So, what were you calling about?"

"Oh yeah, just to see if you wanted to catch a movie tonight. The new *Star Trek* is on at the multiplex, and I know how much you love Chris Pine."

"You are correct in that, but I have to say no. A movie is not in my budget right about now."

"My treat. Come on, I don't wanna go by myself."

"What about Josh?"

"He has to work."

"I can't let you pay for me, Kyle. Movie tickets are ridiculous these days."

"You're worth it. 'Sides, I think you need a little cheering up. How can you resist seeing my perky smile, or my even perkier ass for that matter? Together they are guaranteed to chase all the blues away."

Mark laughed. "Don't think much of yourself, do you? Okay, but soon as I make some money, I'm taking you to the movies and buying you dinner!" He laughed again at the sound of Kyle's infectious whoop and giggle.

"Meet me outside at six. And you might have had the good news by then. That'll mean a celebration. Keeping my fingers, my eyes and my balls all crossed for ya!"

"TMI, Kyle...but I appreciate the thought." He was still smiling when he ended the call. *Thank God for Kyle.* He really was a good friend, always had been since the day they'd met in Fairmont Hills Junior High. Their lives had taken them in different directions over the years, but they'd always remained in touch, either by email or Facebook, and now that they were living in the same city, by phone, text and the occasional meeting for a drink. Kyle worked for an accountancy firm—'*boring as shit, but it pays the bills*'—and shared an apartment with a guy who worked in the law department of the same company.

He'd wanted Mark to come live with them, but Josh, the other guy, hadn't appeared too keen, so Mark had ended up sharing an apartment in Silver Lake with two other out-of-work actors looking for breaks and working as waiters in the meantime.

"So stereotypical," Andrew, one of his future roommates, had said when he'd come to see the apartment. "But what can ya do?"

Mark had also been working as a waiter until recently, but two customers had put paid to that by telling the manager Mark had complained to them about the size of the tip they'd left him. They hadn't left him anything, but Mark hadn't said a word. He guessed the look he'd thrown their penny-pinching faces had said it all. They'd demanded he be fired and the manager had complied like the gutless wonder he was. Mark hadn't cried about it at the time, but a month later the rent and just the basics of a frugal life were taking their toll. And even waiting jobs were hard to find these days. He realized he'd been pinning too many of his hopes on getting the part of a rookie detective in the new cops and robbers TV series that had become a must-watch on Friday nights. Ah well, if he didn't hear anything today he'd call his agent in the morning and ask if he had something else Mark could audition for.

* * * *

He wished he had good news to give Kyle when he met him outside the multiplex. His pint-sized, redheaded friend's expectant smile changed to a frown when Mark gave him a gloomy shake of his head.

"I'm sorry, Mark." Kyle hugged him tight. "What the hell is wrong with them? They couldn't find a hotter rookie cop anywhere else in all of Los Angeles. You'd have been wowing the women, and most of the men, with those devil-may-care looks and sassy attitude. Sometimes you remind me of Rock Hudson in the movie *Captain Lightfoot*. He was never more handsome, in my opinion. You're not as tall, which is a good thing…six feet, just the right height. You won't ever have to stoop."

"Well, thanks, and you should know, I guess. Captain Lightfoot? Never heard of him."

Kyle groaned. At twenty-five, he was a movie buff who knew more about the old movies and stars than probably a lot of the so-called critics. "That's because you don't watch TCM. As an actor, you should watch more of those classic films. They knew how to do it then."

"And they don't now?"

"Some do, but back then the stars had class and kept the scandals where they belong…under the rug."

Mark laughed. "That must be where the phrase rug burn comes from."

"That would come from being on top of the rug." Kyle pulled his iPhone from his pocket, searched for a moment or two then showed Mark the image on the screen. "Captain Lightfoot."

Mark stared at the tall, handsome man in a long, high-collared black coat, his hair artfully tousled to hang over his forehead. Stunning.

"Wow, you think I'm like him?"

"Very much like him, 'cept I think you're even better looking." He giggled and hooked his arm through Mark's as they strolled through the lobby of the giant complex that sported fifteen different theaters, five of them showing the new release, *Star Trek*. "Anyway, I think they're nuts not hiring you. You are so handsome, Mark, you're being wasted on the unemployment line. I wish I knew some people who could help you find the right part in a blockbuster series."

"You're a sweetheart, Kyle, and so good for my ego—crushed as it is right now."

"Something will break, I know it." He gazed up into

Mark's eyes and sighed. "You really belong on the big screen, not TV."

"Kyle."

"I know, it sounds like I'm fan-boying all over the place, but I mean it. I'm a fan, as well as your friend."

They'd reached the ticket office and Kyle slid a credit card toward the cashier. "Two for *Star Trek*, please." Tickets in hand, they made their way to the theater. "Popcorn?"

"Uh..." Mark was hungry, but he really didn't want Kyle spending even more money for the astronomically priced popcorn or sodas.

"That means yes." Kyle headed for the popcorn counter. "Me too. We'll share."

"Thanks, Kyle." Mark was beginning to feel like a freeloader. He had to start making money soon so he could at least pay his way. There weren't too many he knew who were as generous as Kyle.

Ah well... Tomorrow is another day.

* * * *

Barney Coburn, Mark's agent, said he had nothing on the books that would suit Mark 'at the moment'. "Oh, unless you'd be interested in playing a fag in this indie movie I heard about."

Mark growled but said nothing. Barney wasn't particularly homophobic, just damn inappropriate sometimes.

"They're having a hard time casting it, so they're looking around for lesser names, y'know." He chortled, obviously amusing himself. "Couldn't get Brad or Hugh to play, or even Orlando, so... Anyway, what d'ya think?"

"Right now, I'll go for anything. You said 'indie'. So, it's a movie, not television."

"Right, but if it gets any further than HBO, I'll be surprised."

At this point, who cares? Mark thought. *As long as there's a paycheck somewhere, I'll be happy to play a 'fag'. Jeez...*

"Nothing wrong with HBO, Barney."

"You're right, you're right. Okay..." Mark could hear Barney rustle some papers. His desk was always a mess. He'd never heard of using a computer to store information. "Here's the phone number. Got a pen?"

"Yes." Mark wrote down the number Barney recited at him.

"Don't forget to tell 'em I sent ya."

"Of course not."

"Okay then. Good luck, I guess."

Mark called the number as soon as he'd hung up with Barney. A young man answered after two or three rings. "Ron Lester Productions, how may I help you?"

"Uh, yeah, hi. My agent, Barney Coburn, said you are looking for actors for an indie movie...a, uh, a gay character?"

"Oh, yes. Can I have your name please?"

"Mark Henderson."

"And you're a professional actor, Mark?"

"I've done a bunch of repertory, a production of *The Fantasticks* here in LA and I'm waiting to hear about an audition I did for a new TV series. That's it."

"Okay, Mark. I'm Brett, by the way. The producers have meetings all morning, but why don't you drop by with your portfolio, say at two this afternoon? Here's the address..."

As Mark scribbled the address down, he couldn't quite believe it had been that easy. Of course, it meant nothing yet, but just getting to talk to someone producing a movie was a big step in the right direction. He could hardly wait to tell Kyle and his roomies. Even if Barney was right and it was shown on HBO. Shit, some incredible stuff had been aired by HBO—truly amazing shows and movies.

Kyle, start crossing your...uh, fingers.

* * * *

Ron Lester Productions' office was a small affair in a

twelve-story building in Burbank. The young man behind the desk in the front office — Mark presumed he was Brett — scanned Mark from top to toe and everything in between as he stepped inside the small space. Mark was used to this, but it still irritated him that some people could be so obvious and crass.

"Mark Henderson?" Brett threw a fake smile his way. Mark got the funny idea the guy regarded him as some kind of competition. *What's that about?*

"Yes. I brought my portfolio." He handed over the envelope containing his resume and photographs.

"Take a seat. I'll let the boss know you're here." He rose from his desk and sauntered toward a door a few feet away. Brett was wearing a very cool and expensive-looking multicolored shirt and a pair of tight dark-blue jeans.

You have a nice ass...too bad about the personality. Mark shook his head, watching Brett disappear inside the other room. He'd seemed a lot friendlier on the phone. *Wonder what his problem is?*

Brett was back in a couple of minutes. "You can go through." He held the door open.

"Thanks." The room reeked of smoke and the man who stared at him as he entered made Mark's heart sink. No way was this man a film producer. Fat and balding, a cigarette drooping from his lips, he looked like a reject from a bad B movie. He dropped Mark's photographs onto his desk and leaned back in his chair, his big stomach to the fore. Mark tried not to flinch.

"Ron Lester," the man said. "So, you want to be considered for a part in this movie, *Burning Hearts*? You have to play gay, y'know."

"That's all right."

Lester nodded. "Take a seat."

"Are you the producer?" Mark asked as he sat opposite Lester.

"No. I'm not the one with the money, just the one who finds the talent. The producers have run out of ideas about who to cast in one of the gay roles. They had some guy, can't remember his name... B-list most likely. Anyway, he backed off the other day. Left them high and dry. A lotta actors don't want to be seen doin' that kinda stuff."

"Really? I would've thought these days that kind of stigma was passé."

Lester blew out a huge cloud of smoke that stung Mark's eyes. "Ha, you think? Believe me, some of those that have tried it have suffered after." He reeled off a few names. "Those guys have a hard time getting parts anymore. Have to go auditioning for stage work. Anyway, they are pretty desperate and you don't have a lot to lose. Right?"

Gee, thanks...

"You look good..." Lester's small eyes glinted and Mark tensed involuntarily, but the big man didn't move from his chair. "I'll set up an appointment with Richard Harley and his associates. They're the ones with the money. Why the hell they want to do this movie is beyond me, but hey, it's their money."

"Thank you," Mark said.

"You have more of these?" Lester pointed at Mark's photographs.

"Yes."

"Take another set with you when you go see Harley. I'll keep these in case I have something else I think you'd be good for. Okay?"

"Yes, thanks. You'll call me then?"

Lester nodded, causing his chins to wobble. "Probably tomorrow. Keep your day free. If I can get you an appointment, be ready to go. Oh, and they'll probably want to see you shirtless, just so you know."

As Mark passed Brett's desk on his way out, Brett asked, "How'd it go?"

"Pretty good, I think. He's setting up a meeting with the producers for me, maybe tomorrow. See if I'm what they're looking for."

"Huh, he has what they're *looking* for right here, but the

son of a bitch won't let me audition."

Oh, so that's the problem. "I'm sorry."

"That's what happens when you work for your dad." Brett sighed. He had a cute pout, but he seemed really dejected and Mark did feel sorry for him. "He can't see me doing anything but this shit. No matter that I studied drama in high school, took acting classes, he just won't let me near an audition."

Ouch. "Why don't you contact the producers yourself? You must have their numbers."

Brett jerked his thumb at his father's office door. "He said he'd kick my ass if I did." He finally managed a more sincere smile. "I need this ass for better things."

Mark chuckled. "Well, take care, and thanks for your help in getting me this far."

"Welcome. Sorry I was a bit rude earlier. It just pisses me off that he can't see I have more to offer than just this." He gestured around the office as if to emphasize his lot in life.

"I hear you. Anyway, thanks again." Mark held out his hand and Brett shook it somewhat sheepishly. "See you around."

"Yeah, look forward to it. And good luck tomorrow."

* * * *

Mark was both amused and puzzled when he left Ron Lester's office. He wondered why a legit movie company would use someone like Lester to procure actors. The guy seemed to know the business, but his office screamed small-time. He couldn't see the likes of George Clooney or Hugh Jackman ever setting a foot near the place. Brett, once he'd gotten over his moody, was the only one who'd appeared to be remotely professional and dressed the part. The shirt and the designer jeans that had showcased his butt so well must have cost him a bundle. Was his dad paying him that well? Or maybe he just liked nice clothes to make up for what he saw as a shitty job.

Okay, so he was one more step closer to getting this part. No matter how small or controversial it was, he'd take it if it was offered to him, and he'd do the best he could to make it worthwhile. As he walked to his car, he pulled out his cell and punched in Kyle's speed dial number. He'd still be at work, but he could leave him a message.

"Hi, handsome." Kyle's chirpy voice always made Mark smile.

"I thought you might be busy so I was going to leave a message."

"Not necessary. I'm on a break. What's up?"

"Just thought I'd let you know I have a chance at a part in an indie movie. I have an appointment, hopefully tomorrow, to meet the producers."

"Yay!" Kyle's yell made Mark jerk the phone away from his ear.

"Ouch! Your enthusiasm is appreciated, but I need my eardrum."

They laughed together. "That is so great, Mark. This could be it for you."

"I sure hope so." *Yeah, but I was full of hope the other day.* "Keep everything crossed for me again."

"Will do."

"What are you up to tonight?"

"Uh, believe it or not, but Josh asked me out—on a *date*."

Mark almost dropped his phone. "Josh? But you said you didn't know if he was gay or not."

"He tends to hide it well because of his job, he says. The old dude that runs the law department where we work is a major homophobe, so he has to be low-key. Thank God I don't work in there. Josh says being careful kinda seeps into his everyday life. He wasn't trying to hide it from me, it's just the way he is. And he is a fox, all that floppy hair and steely blue eyes, so I said yes."

Climbing into his car, Mark laughed. "Well, I hope you have a good time. I'll call you tomorrow after my audition. You can give me the scoop then."

So that's why Josh didn't want me sharing the apartment. He had his eye on Kyle and didn't want any competition. Stern and serious Josh and perky, funny Kyle — what a combination. It might just be a partnership made in Heaven.

* * * *

Andrew, one of his roommates, was home when he got back to the apartment. A tall, willowy blond with a ready smile, Andrew was the roomie he got along with. The other, Perry, who was from the UK, was okay, but a bit of a bighead even though he was in the same boat as the rest of them.

"How was your day?" Andrew asked Mark.

"Not bad. I may have a part in an indie movie. I'll know something tomorrow."

"That is fantastic!" Andrew's smile was sincere and the hug he gave Mark felt warm and genuine. "I am so fuckin' jealous! No, I'm not." Andrew laughed. "Yes, I am, but I wish you all the best. Can't wait to see you on the big screen."

"Or the small, as the case may be. My agent seems to think it might be picked up by HBO."

"HBO's a big deal. Hey…" Andrew ran into the kitchen. "We need a drink to celebrate." He produced a bottle of chardonnay from the fridge and waved it at Mark. "It's not champagne, but it'll do, right?"

"What's all the racket about?" Perry peered at them from the hallway, a pissed-off expression on his otherwise handsome face. He was wearing only boxers and his dark-brown hair had flopped over his eyes. He pushed at it impatiently as he glared at them. "I was trying to take a nap." Older than both Mark and Andrew, Perry was in good shape, and despite his sour expression, he was an attractive man.

"Mark's gonna be a movie star and we're celebrating, sourpuss," Andrew yelled at him.

Perry frowned. "A movie *star*?" He pronounced it 'stawr'.

"Well, it's an indie movie," Mark told him, "and I don't actually have the part yet. Andrew's kinda jumping the gun."

"Huh, that's more like it." Perry slouched over to the kitchen and grabbed one of the glasses Andrew was filling with wine. "When will you know?" he asked after taking a long sip.

"Hopefully tomorrow."

Andrew handed Mark a chilled glass then clinked his own against Mark's. "Good luck. You should get it with your looks alone. The camera will love you."

"Thanks, Andrew."

Perry snorted. "Give it up, Andy. You're not his type." His English accent made the condescension in his tone even more marked.

"Hey, that's not very nice." Andrew looked suitably hurt.

Mark stared at Perry. "How do you know what my type is?"

"I don't, but I imagine it's not a tall skinny blond who waits tables and hasn't a penny in the bank."

"That is so insulting, Perry." Now Andrew sounded mad. "As if you're doing any better. You wait tables too, and you haven't been in a show in decades. You're thirty years old and have nothing to show for it."

"Guys!" Mark glared at them both. "Cut it out. Perry, you should apologize to Andrew. That was uncalled for."

"And what *she* said wasn't?" Perry threw back the rest of his wine then stomped off to his room, slamming the door behind him.

"I hate it when he acts like that." Andrew slumped onto the couch. "He tries to be so macho when he's nothing but a petty bitch."

Mark sighed. He so did not want to be in the middle of a roomie fight. "You guys will get over it," he said carefully. "You've known each other a long time."

"Too long." Andrew's eyes glistened as he gazed at Mark.

"Don't know why I've stuck around, really. He'll never see me as anyone but the skinny blond he can wrap around his little finger. What I said about having nothing to show for his age? He won't forgive me for that for a long time."

Before Mark could comment, Andrew finished his wine then rose from the couch and put his glass in the kitchen sink. "I think I'll go watch TV in my room. Good luck tomorrow. I hope you get the part. One of us needs a fucking break."

* * * *

Mark found it hard to sleep that night. Partly, he figured, because of what might or might not happen tomorrow, and partly because the fight between Andrew and Perry had brought back some uncomfortable memories of the last time he'd spoken to Corey, his ex. That had been a lot worse than the spat between his roomies. Mark punched his pillow a few times then sank back down into it, trying to erase the thoughts swirling through his mind. No such luck. Corey's face swam in his vision behind his closed eyelids—that wholesome farm boy look he exuded even though he'd been born and raised in the city. That sunny smile, the perfect teeth and the bluest of eyes. Shining eyes that hid the darkness inside, the need to cause hurt to the ones who loved him the most.

Mark had been one of those who had loved Corey. Had loved him with all his heart and soul. He'd been warned. He couldn't deny it, but those warnings had sounded like so much jealousy and sour grapes as far as he'd been concerned. His other friends were jealous, that was it, he'd thought at the time. Jealous that he had landed what everyone else wanted. The handsome college football hero, best quarterback Spokane's Fairmont Hills team had ever produced. Corey Barnett...

When Mark really wanted to torture himself, he'd lie in bed and remember what Corey's body had felt like under his caressing hands. All that corded muscle covered by smooth, silky skin, the thick golden hair that he longed to run his fingers through after the infrequent sex—if Corey didn't find some excuse or other to pull away a few moments after he'd come. Not a cuddler or a kisser, Corey. Not a nice guy, either. A son of a bitch, really. If Andrew felt hurt after what Perry had said to him, he'd have withered and died under Corey's verbal assaults.

Mark and everyone else knew what was wrong with Corey. There was no easy fix for bipolar disorder, and with someone like Corey, who refused to take his meds on principle, there was no controlling it, or him. Eventually he'd lashed out at Mark one time too many. The love that had blinded Mark to Corey's abuse had suddenly fallen away and in front of his eyes all he had seen had been an ugly, sneering, contemptible human being who'd deserved nothing more than a punch in the face. After that, Mark had left town and headed to Los Angeles, hoping to lose himself in the overcrowded city and pursue his dream of a career in acting.

"And here I am," Mark said to the ceiling. "Two years later, still dreaming, and until a week ago, waiting tables, just like Penny in *The Big Bang Theory*...only she had a decent boyfriend." He chuckled to himself. *Yeah, Mark... It's good you can still laugh. Laughter takes away the hurt, so they say. Funny how it's not working.*

"Shit." He turned onto his side and mumbled, "Go the fuck to sleep."

Chapter Two

The following day, Mark didn't dare stray too far from his cell phone. When he didn't have it in his pocket or on the kitchen table while he had breakfast, he took it into the bathroom while he showered. By noon he was feeling despondent, by two, definitely mopey and at three, almost suicidal. At three-thirty his phone chimed.

"Mark Henderson."

"Hello, Mark, this is Richard Harley."

Yes! Oh. My. God. "Oh, hi, Mr. Harley. Uh…" *Shit, your voice sounds like a two year old's.*

"Ron Lester called me and said he thinks you might be right for a part in my upcoming movie. I'd like to meet with you and discuss that if you're interested."

Mark cleared his throat before answering. "Yes, that would be great. I am very interested."

"Excellent." Harley's voice was slightly accented. *British, Australian?* Mark wasn't sure. "I'll be in my office in about an hour. Can you meet me there?"

"Of course. In an hour?"

"Yes." Harley rattled off an address on Sunset Boulevard then added, "See you in an hour, Mark. Bye for now."

"Bye." Mark found he couldn't move. Nor could he quite believe that the guy had called and was actually considering him for the part. Well, wanted to meet with him about the part. *Same thing, right?* He forced himself to his feet and made for his bedroom.

Choosing the right clothes was important. He wanted to impress, after all, but a suit and tie might be too much. He wished he knew what the part was, what kind of character he'd be auditioning for—a young gay man, that was as much as he knew. Well, he was a young gay man, so he would wear what most gay guys wore, unless they were going on an interview. *'Cause that's what this is, right?* An interview, so he should look smart. No jeans. Slacks and a button-down shirt? He should shave again, but maybe Harley wanted someone with a bit of a shadow. Shit, he could go on and on guessing what Richard Harley might want. He just had to show up, looking as good as Kyle said he did, and hope for the best.

He went to his closet and pulled a pair of his tightest jeans off their hanger.

* * * *

Light in the Forest Productions was housed in a much fancier space than Ron Lester Productions. That gave Mark's hopes a boost, along with the familiar flutter of nerves in his stomach whenever he went for an audition. He knocked on the glass-paned door then pushed it open. A tall, silver-haired man stood behind a desk in the center of the room, scanning some papers he held in his hand. He looked up and smiled at Mark.

"Come on in. Mark, I presume. I'm Richard Harley."

"Pleased to meet you, sir." Mark shook the proffered hand and met Harley's appraising stare head-on. No point in trying to appear to be coy. He felt relieved on seeing the man was dressed casually in jeans and a polo shirt. The blue denim shirt Mark had chosen to wear didn't feel out of place.

"You brought your portfolio?"

"Yes." Mark handed it over.

"Take a seat while I go through this."

There was silence for a few minutes and Mark glanced around the well-appointed office that was, thankfully, smoke free. Late-afternoon sunlight cast slivers of gold across the beige carpeting and glinted on the glass-and-chrome furniture placed in two groups at the far end of the room. Obviously an office and meeting room combination, with no sign of a receptionist's desk. Mark wondered if Harley took care of everything…

"Fairly impressive amount of stage work," Harley said finally, "but no experience in film."

"No, not yet, anyway."

"I like your headshots. You're extremely photogenic."

"Thank you." Mark hoped that was a good thing. *For a movie, you should be photogenic, right?*

Harley smiled and pushed a script toward Mark. "I hope you don't mind if I cut right to the chase here. The actor we were considering for the role reneged after stringing us along for over a month. We're under considerable time constraints due to our limited budget. So, page eleven, the character named Peter, read me his first line."

Wow, he doesn't waste any time. Mark willed his hands not to shake as he turned the pages to the appropriate spot. "Uh…" There wasn't even a brief character description. He did a quick scan of the action and the dialog underneath.

Detective Jeff Hollister interrupts Peter while he's working on a portrait in his studio. Peter turns from his easel and stares at Jeff.

"Okay, Mark. When you're ready."

Mark took a deep breath and began to read…

Peter: Just for the record, what is it about me that makes you think I had anything to do with blackmailing Samantha Goodall? I told you last time we talked that I barely knew the woman, now you're acting like I'm the only suspect. Let's get this straight once and for all, I did not blackmail her, nor did I kill her.

"Not bad," Harley said. "Okay, now read it again, this time with emphasis on the last line. Try to sound pissed off."

Mark reread the lines, throwing a biting inflection into the last few words.

Harley nodded. "Better, good in fact. Okay, I'll read the next line, that's Jeff the detective's, and you pick it up from there. I'll also read the action descriptions so you'll understand what's going on."

"Okay."

Jeff: Has anyone told you you're kind of hot when you get all defensive?

Peter: Detective, you are not scoring any brownie points with me using that type of approach. Apart from being inappropriate, it's cheesy at best.

Jeff: *He takes a step or two closer to Peter.* Cheesy, huh? *He laughs.* I guess I'll have to improve my pick-up lines. How about this? *He grabs Peter and kisses him. Peter starts to push him away, but falters under the pressure of Jeff's lips. He returns the kiss.*

Peter *(Slightly out of breath)*: I'd say that was a marked improvement. You interrogate all your suspects like this?

"That's pretty good, Mark." Harley leaned back in his chair and stared at him for a long minute or two. Long enough for Mark's nerves to kick in again. "I think you have the looks for the part, and for a first reading, you did well. The actor playing Jeff Hollander, the detective, is Evan Ericson. You heard of him?"

Mark shook his head. "No."

"He's new to mainstream movies. He was involved in the gay porn industry for a time, but he wants to put that behind him and legitimize his career. He's actually a pretty decent actor, much better than some of those guys in porn who are unfortunate enough to be asked to say actual lines." Harley grinned and rifled through a file drawer for a moment before handing Mark a photograph.

Mark's eyes widened. The guy was hot and he looked vaguely familiar. "Oh…" He chuckled. "I think I may have seen him in a porn movie. A friend of mine has quite a collection. I just didn't recognize the name."

"His porn name was Dean Masters."

"Oh, right. I have heard of him, vaguely."

"Anyway, I'd like you to meet him, see what kind of chemistry you have together. If you connect, I'll offer you the part after you have a screen test, and we can discuss details. Is that okay?"

"Of course." Mark had to work hard to control his impulse to start jumping up and down with excitement.

"I have to tell you that we could be taking a bit of a risk using Evan," Harley said. "Porn isn't an easy thing to shake off, and no doubt when the word gets out about his past, some people will take issue with it. However, I'm of the opinion that he's a good enough actor that when the critics actually see his work, they'll concentrate on that and not what he used to do."

"And it's all publicity, right?"

"Exactly. Okay, Mark. I'll give Evan a call and see if he's free to come meet you. I told him I was auditioning you, so I know he'll be anxious to hear the outcome. He's eager to do this movie." He picked up his cell and punched in a number.

"Evan? Hey, Richard Harley. I have Mark Henderson, the actor I told you about, here in the office. I'd like you to meet with him and trade some lines. Can you come over now? Good. See you in about a half hour." He smiled at Mark. "On his way over. Let's take another look at the script while we're waiting."

Mark opened the binder containing the script again and noticed Harley's name under the title. "Oh, you wrote this, Mr. Harley?"

"Call me Richard. Yes, and it's been the usual blood, sweat and tears trying to get it made into a movie. I managed to get a group of investors to help with the cost, but I have a chunk of my own money tied up in it too, so, as you can imagine, I'm anxious that it be a success."

Mark could well understand the sentiment. If he got the part, he'd wish it to be the movie of the year.

* * * *

When Evan Ericson walked into the office, Mark jumped to his feet and instantly regretted it. His knees almost gave out and he was sure his mouth was hanging open. The man's photograph did no justice whatsoever to the real McCoy. He was simply amazing. A shock of thick blond hair crowned his head and curled around his ears. Silver-gray eyes gazed at Mark from under feathered eyebrows, and his mouth... *Jeez.* Mark's breath caught in his throat as Evan's full lips peeled back in a smile that revealed perfectly white, straight teeth.

"Hi, there...you must be Mark." He held his hand out, strong and steady.

"Y-yes. Pleased to meet you."

"Likewise." His grip was warm and his eyes when they met Mark's held just a hint of mischief. Evan Ericson's charisma was unmistakable, it poured off him in waves, and Mark was sure most anyone who met him would feel it as palpably as Mark now did.

"We've been going over the script," Richard said, effectively breaking the spell Mark felt Evan had cast over him.

"Great. What d'you think, Mark?"

"I-it's good, really good." Mark willed himself to pull it together, but shit, the guy was just so...incredible. "I already like the scene I read with Mr...uh, Richard."

"Yeah, me too. It's cool the way uptight Peter gets his world rocked...by me."

His grin was infectious and helped Mark relax somewhat.

"Well, you both look good together," Richard said, "so take a few minutes to get to know each other. I'll be right back."

Left alone, Mark and Evan exchanged smiles, then Evan pointed over to the far end of the room. "Let's sit over there."

Mark followed Evan, taking advantage of the view of the

guy's toned body and sweet ass. Evan's baggy shirt couldn't hide the breadth of his shoulders or the trimness of his waist and his jeans showcased his sculpted butt beautifully. *He must be totally astounding naked*, Mark thought, and immediately felt a strong pulse in his groin. Evan sprawled on a leather couch and put his feet up on one of the chrome-and-glass tables. He patted the cushion next to him.

"Don't be shy." Evan's smile was all tease. "If you get the part, we're going to get real close in the movie."

"Right." He sat primly a couple of feet away from Evan and cleared his throat.

Evan chuckled. "Did Richard tell you what I used to do in movies?"

Mark nodded. "Porn."

"Hope that doesn't bother you."

"Not at all." He glanced at Evan. "As a matter of fact…"

"You've seen 'em."

"Just one. At a friend's."

"Ha. Amazing how many times I've been told that. 'Oh no, I didn't buy it. I saw it at a friend's place'."

"Well, it happens to be true." Mark felt his face grow hot. "I don't watch that much porn, but my friend—"

"Hey, it's okay. Just teasin' ya." He gazed at Mark from under his ridiculously long lashes. "So, what have you done?"

"Mostly stage work. I started out in college theatre, then Summer Stock, and I managed to get a part in a production of *The Fantasticks* when I came to LA. But since then it's been rough, to tell you the truth. I've been waiting tables. I was up for a part in a new TV series, but I haven't heard back from them, so…that's it. My career in a nutshell. A very small nut."

"Well, this could be the break we both deserve," Evan said.

"What made you do porn movies, if you don't mind me asking?"

"Money. I had a career in modeling for several years,

but when that dried up I realized I hadn't prepared for unemployment. I have a mortgage, a car payment, and I want to keep what I have, so I grabbed at what was offered to me."

"It's hard for me to believe your modeling career dried up. You are so..." Mark hesitated for a moment. "Uh, well I'm sure it's not news to you that you're a beautiful guy. I would've thought the fashion houses would have been clamoring for your look."

"That's nice of you to say, but I'm afraid I got a bit of a bad-boy reputation. Drugs can make you unreliable."

"Oh."

"I'm over that shit now, though. Learned my lesson the hard way. Thing is, I also learned not to hold grudges, not to be bitter. Life's too short." Evan dropped his feet off the table and stretched out his long legs in front of him, and Mark looked quickly away from the very noticeable bulge behind Evan's zipper. "So, music?" Evan asked. "You like music?"

Mark chuckled. "I'm afraid I am the stereotypical gay male. I love Broadway tunes and Lady Gaga."

"I like her and Adele, but mostly I listen to classical guitar."

"Really?"

Evan nodded. "When we know each other better I'll have you listen to one of Rodrigo's Guitar Concertos...my favorite." His smile was nothing if not flirtatious. "Music to make love to, for sure."

Before Mark could react in any way at all to that, Harley entered the office carrying a six-pack of beer. "Okay, guys, come have a drink, then we'll get started. Had enough time to bond?"

Evan stood and Mark followed. "I think we're on the same page." He grabbed two beers, handed one to Mark and cracked his open. "What d'you want us to read?"

"The part where you, as Jeff, and Peter—or Mark in this case—first declare their attraction for each other." He handed Mark his script.

"I know the lines," Evan said. "Okay…" He tapped Mark's beer can with his. "Here's to us."

"To us." Mark smiled.

They took long swallows of their beers then Evan said, "So let's do it."

Harley beamed at them. "Page eleven, again, Mark. You're at your easel, you hear Jeff come into your studio and you turn to face him. Okay?"

"Okay." He took a moment then did a half turn toward Evan.

"Just for the record, what is it about me that makes you think I had anything to do with blackmailing Samantha Goodall? I told you last time we talked that I barely knew the woman, now you're acting like I'm the only suspect. Let's get this straight once and for all, I did not blackmail her, nor did I kill her!"

Evan's smile was as sexy as sin. "Has anyone told you you're kind of hot when you get all defensive?"

Mark raised an eyebrow. "Detective, you are not scoring any brownie points with me using that type of approach. Apart from it being inappropriate, it's cheesy at best."

Evan stepped close to Mark. "Cheesy, huh?" He laughed, moved even closer and started to undo the buttons on Mark's shirt. "I guess I'll have to improve my pick-up lines. How about this?" He ripped Mark's shirt open and pulled him into his arms.

Mark's mouth was already open from the shock of Evan's unscripted move when Evan kissed him. Evan's tongue glided effortlessly between Mark's parted lips.

Holy shit! Mark felt as if his brain had been zapped by the force of Evan's kiss. This time his knees did buckle and the script he'd been holding fell from his hand. He pressed himself against Evan for support, holding on to him with all his might, returning the kiss with a fervor he didn't know he had in him. His cock sprang to life inside his briefs and he gasped into Evan's mouth when he felt a hard, thick erection slide over his. *Christ, we're practically rutting on each other!*

He almost cried when Evan broke the kiss. Evan's gray eyes held a teasing light. "You forgot your next line?"

What the fuck was it? Something about being out of breath. That bit he could do. Evan had practically stolen every bit of oxygen from his lungs.

"I'd say that was a marked improvement," he said, his voice shaky with emotion. "You interrogate all your suspects like this?"

"Fucking fabulous!" Richard's shout made Mark jump. He'd completely forgotten the man was in the room with them. "That is going to set the screen on fire! Great job, guys. Mark, as far as I'm concerned, you have the part. Right, Evan?"

"Oh, yes." Evan still had his arms around Mark. He gazed at him from hooded, sexy eyes. "Totally right."

Richard seemed to be as excited as Mark. "I'll have your screen test with Charles Bennet, our director, set up for tomorrow morning. I'll text you with the time, okay? It'll be at Woodside Studios in Burbank, actually on Burbank Boulevard. You know it?"

"I can find it."

"Okay, great." Richard held out his hand and Mark had to free himself from Evan's arms before he could shake it. "See you tomorrow then, Mark."

* * * *

Mark and Evan took the elevator from Harley's office to the parking garage together. "I want to thank you," Mark said.

"For what?"

"For making that audition so easy for me."

"Hey, I enjoyed it. You're a great kisser, y'know." He grinned at Mark. "And a pretty good actor."

"Just pretty good?" Mark met Evan's mischievous smile

with one of his own.

"*Very* good, then. You wanna go for a drink? We should take some time to get to know each other better." He glanced at his watch, a slim affair with a black face and tiny diamonds depicting the numbers.

"Beautiful watch," Mark said.

"Spoils of the game," Evan told him, his smile faintly wry. "But you don't want to hear about that. So, drink?"

"Yes, that would be nice."

Evan looked at him, his expression serious for once. "You're a sweet guy, Mark. I like you."

"I like you too. That's a good thing, right?" The elevator doors slid open and they stepped out.

"Yeah, a good thing." Evan's smile was back. "We're gonna be pretty tight in some of the scenes, so it's definitely good that we like each other."

Pretty tight... Mark couldn't wait. "Uh, where d'you want to go?"

"The Abbey's pretty close. Meet you there?"

"Okay. See you in a few."

Mark made his way to his car and couldn't help but peek to see what Evan was driving. *Shit... An Audi 500 Sportster.* He almost waited until Evan had driven off so he couldn't see Mark's beat-up Oldsmobile, but what was the point when he'd see it later at the bar anyway? Sighing, he climbed inside and returned Evan's wave as he sped out of the garage.

So, porn must pay. Or maybe he'd made money in other ways—residuals from his modeling career, perhaps. *Whatever, it's not any of your business.* Evan had proven himself to be a really nice guy, and not at all selfish like he'd known some actors to be. The way he'd enhanced that scene between them had been incredible, and hot as hell.

Evan thinks I'm a great kisser, but it was really all him.

He was hard again just thinking about it. He could still feel Evan's lips on his, Evan's scent, which had ratcheted up Mark's visceral reaction to that kiss. He'd been hard and so had Evan, which had made it all that more real. That's what it was—a real attraction between them. The chemistry that Harley wanted, it was there without a doubt, and Mark wondered just where it might take them both. If they were to be more than just actors working together, he'd be up for that, no two ways about it.

* * * *

He arrived at the bar's parking lot just behind Evan, who'd waited for him so they could walk in together. As usual, the Abbey was busy, loud and crowded, and he noticed most of the patrons turning to stare as they made their way to the bar.

"You're creating quite a stir," he murmured in Evan's ear.

"The stir's about you, I think."

Mark snorted. "What'll it be?"

"Stella on tap, thanks…and they're on me. I asked you out. And don't be so quick to dismiss the fact that you are one hot guy," Evan told him. "I'm sure you've left a trail of broken hearts behind you in—where are you from?"

"Spokane, Washington, and believe me, there are no broken hearts. Only a broken nose."

"Not yours." Evan did a quick scan of Mark's nose then touched it lightly on the tip with his finger. "No, in perfect shape."

Mark grinned. "No, not mine."

"There's a story in there that I'm dying to hear."

The smiling bartender delivered their drinks and Evan slipped him a twenty. He picked up the foaming glasses then he and Mark headed for a corner of the bar, Evan saying 'hi' to two or three people on the way. They found one of the last few remaining tables and sat side by side on a padded bench.

Evan raised his glass. "Here's to you, Mark, and to success for both of us in our first movie together."

"I'll drink to that," Mark said. "Wait, you said our first

movie together. You think there might be another?"

Evan winked. "It is my fervent hope."

"I'll drink to that too." They took long, heartfelt swallows of their beers.

"So…" Evan wiped the foam from his lips with the back of his hand, "tell me the broken nose story."

Mark sighed. "I don't know if I should. It's not something I'm proud of, really. It was a bad part of my life. Still keeps me awake some nights thinking about it."

Evan tapped Mark's arm lightly. "Maybe if you shared it would help exorcise the sleepless nights. Have you told anyone about it?"

"My friend Kyle. He and I go back a while. We haven't kept much from each other over the years."

"I'm jealous of him already."

Mark raised his eyebrows. "You are?"

"Just kidding. I'm glad you have someone you can talk to."

"You don't?"

"It's amazing how many friends desert you when your own luck goes south." Evan grimaced. "Now I sound like I'm whining, and I don't mean to. I still have a couple of friends."

"Doesn't sound like whining to me. Sometimes friends can disappoint you, but it's up to us to see beyond that, I think."

Evan nodded. "So, the guy with the broken nose disappointed you?"

Mark laughed. "You're not going to give up on that, are you?"

"It's okay if you don't want to talk about it." Evan took another long swallow of his beer.

"Okay — the short version. I was in love with a guy, Corey Barnett, a tall, handsome, hung quarterback. Everything I wasn't. I was your typical nerd, skinny, naïve, not at all into sports, but I went to see every game and practice Corey was in. We were together for two years — or rather, I should say,

I followed him about for two years and he'd occasionally let me blow him. That was the extent of his feelings for me. He would never acknowledge me when he was with his friends. Too afraid that his knowing me would brand him as a 'faggot'. I'm sure you know the type."

Evan shrugged. "They're everywhere – even in pornland."

"Really?"

"Yeah. I met some of the biggest homophobes during the time I made those movies. Those straight gay-for-pay guys – ugh. They'll stick it up a guy's ass, come all over you, but the whole time their eyes are dead. They try not to look at you. It's like fucking a zombie. And don't even talk about the kissing." He shuddered then laughed. "Like sticking your tongue into a dead fish's mouth."

Mark laughed. "I never could quite understand how they get hard for a guy if they're straight. Damned if I could for a woman."

Evan chuckled. "You're that example of the one hundred percent gay man."

"You've slept with women?"

"Sure, back in college, but not since then. I'm pretty much your complete homo now."

Mark laughed again. He was enjoying Evan's company, even though they'd veered into a subject Mark was still not too comfortable with.

"Anyway, back to your quarterback…"

"Yeah, I thought I'd managed to change the subject."

"Not on your life. I want to hear how he got that broken nose."

"Easy. Corey was nuts, verbally and physically abusive. Bipolar and wouldn't take his meds. He and his dad got into it on numerous occasions. His mother was scared to death of him. I was the only one who thought I saw the real Corey – the guy who would whisper dirty stuff in my ear when we were alone and make it sound like he really cared for me, really wanted me in his life. The day I told him I loved him, he laughed so goddamn hard I thought he was going to have a heart attack. He literally came close to throwing up."

"My God."

"Yeah, I should've known to shut the fuck up after that, but shithead here thought I could change him. If I showed that I really did love him, he might be a better person. What a schmuck I was. Young and stupid." Mark paused to sip his beer then ended up draining the glass.

"Like another?"

"I shouldn't. Driving…"

"I live about a block from here." Evan's eyes gleamed as he added, "You could come back to my place so you won't have to drive. Is there anyone waiting for you at home?"

Mark grinned. "Was that a way to find out if I was single or not?"

"Are you? Single or not?"

"Yep, single."

"Me too, so come home with me. Be single with me. We don't have to do anything other than talk." He smiled and rubbed Mark's arm. "I have beer there also."

"Now you're talking."

Evan laughed. "Let's go."

Chapter Three

"Nice place," Mark said, looking around Evan's apartment. The polished dark wood floors were accented by a couple of brightly patterned rugs, one in front of an over-stuffed leather couch, the other under a dining table and chairs. Two large prints that appeared to be impressionist landscapes hung on the wall behind the couch. A series of shelves filled with books, CDs and a TV set took up another wall. He walked over to the window and stared out at the darkening sky, the sun just a faint glow in the distance. "I like that you have a view of the park too."

"Yeah, I was lucky with the location. I'll get you a beer."

Mark followed him into the kitchen, once again getting what was fast becoming his even more favorite view—Evan's ass. Mark felt a familiar stirring in his groin when Evan bent over to extract the beer from the fridge.

"You okay?" Evan asked, handing him a bottle. "Your eyes are a little glazed."

Mark averted said eyes from Evan's. "I'm fine." He clinked his bottle against Evan's. "Cheers."

"Cheers. So, come sit and tell me the rest. Sorry by the way, you had to park on the street. But it's a fairly decent neighborhood."

"Don't worry. No one's going to steal that piece of junk."

They settled on the couch and Evan stared at Mark expectantly.

Mark groaned. "Do we have to do this?"

"Yes." Evan chuckled. "You can't leave me hanging now."

Mark smiled at the double entendre. "Okay, here goes. Corey got into a fight with his dad. Huge fucking fight. His mother called the police, but she got her story screwed up and it ended up with Corey's dad getting arrested, even though he was bleeding badly from a cut on his head. Corey called me, said he wanted to meet up. He was crying. I'd never heard or seen him do that before. So of course I went out to meet him, in a park near his house. He was a mess. Told me he was going to kill his dad. I asked what the fight was about. Someone his dad worked with had told him there was a rumor going about that Corey was gay.

"He'd been seen with 'that Henderson kid' — me — and a couple of other guys we ran around with. He was still crying and I put my arm around his shoulders to comfort him, and then I did the impermissible — I kissed him on his cheek. He went nuts, screamed at me to get the fuck away from him, that it was all my fault for being such a fucking pansy and that I had tainted his life with my faggot ways. It's funny, because maybe a week or so before he'd told me the only reason he let me suck his cock was because I didn't look like a queer, that I was handsome and quite manly, even though I was a fairy."

"Jesus, Mark…" Evan stared at him, a frown creasing his forehead. "Why did you ever have anything to do with this creep?"

Mark looked away, swiping at the tears that burned his eyes with the back of his hand. It amazed him that even after two years, the memory of that time was still painful. "That's a really good question, Evan, and the answer is, I really don't know why. He was beautiful on the outside, and everything I hated on the inside. He had a black soul. At the time, I blamed his parents for most of his problems, but now I know it wasn't only their fault. Corey was sick, and they couldn't deal with it. Anyway, I realized I couldn't help him at that moment, so I said something to the effect of I'll talk to you when you're not so mad at me and the world. Something like that. He went batshit crazy then. Screaming, literally screaming at me, calling me all the most vile things. He acted like he was demented. Like he would kill me at any moment. There were people walking in the park. They started to come over, I guess to check out what this madman was doing.

"I turned to go and he grabbed me by the shoulder really hard. Corey was a big guy, and strong, and when he was riled up like that, he didn't know how to control himself. When he was upset, he always looked like there was something lethal inside him ready to burst free and lash out at whoever was closest.

"I saw him pull his fist back ready to smash my face in — and just then somebody yelled, 'Cut that out' and I knew I had to stop him. He hesitated when that person yelled, and I took a shot. I guess I was mad too, because the punch I threw was a lot harder than I'd ever thrown before. I hit him right on his nose. I could hear the cartilage break and blood spurted everywhere. He howled like a banshee and fell on the ground writhing all over the place like a beached whale.

"The guy who'd yelled told me to get the hell away while he called the police on his cell. So I did. The next day I heard Corey had been arrested. This being the second time on the same night that the cops had been to see him, plus this time his mother got her head together, they locked Corey up and let his dad go home."

"Wow, that is quite the story. I imagine it didn't end right there."

"Oh no, but I'd learned my lesson. As much as he'd hurt me in the past, this time I knew it had to be over. I had to get as far away from him as possible. I told my parents I was leaving, going to LA, see if I could do what I'd wanted to for years all through high school and college — make something of myself as an actor. They didn't take too kindly to the idea. Said I'd be back looking foolish. Yeah, thanks for the encouragement, Mom and Dad. They never had approved of my urge to be an actor — thought it was too gay, something that their religion frowns upon. I haven't been back. There's nothing there for me. My best friend,

Kyle, had left Spokane by then and told me he was moving to LA, so it seemed like a good move for me too."

"What happened to Broken Nose?"

"He ended up in jail about two months after I left. Another fight with his father, and this time his old man asked the judge to throw the book at him. Probably still inside."

Mark gulped at the last of his beer and fell back against the couch pillows, enjoying the buzz from the alcohol. *Funny how bottled beer always acts quicker than the draft,* he thought. On him, anyway. He turned to smile at Evan, not in the least surprised to see he had moved closer, so close that their thighs touched. The heat that touch generated seemed to envelope Mark's whole body, hardening his cock and filling him with a longing for an even more intimate closeness.

Evan leaned in and brushed his lips over Mark's. "I think," he murmured, "that you need something, or someone, to take your mind off the past and let you enjoy the present… and maybe even the future."

"I'd like that." Mark opened to him and their tongues glided together, gently at first, almost tentative in their exploration of each other's mouths. This close up, Mark could see tiny blue shards in the gray of Evan's eyes. *Beautiful…* He moaned softly and Evan slipped his arms around him, pulling him into a warm, hard embrace. Their kiss deepened, hot, intense. The logical part of Mark's mind went fuzzy, overcome with lust and the unbelievably erotic things Evan's tongue was doing inside his mouth.

He sank into the couch's cushions, Evan's weight now fully on top of him, their bodies pressed together from mouth to crotch. Mark's first instinct was to cup Evan's amazing ass with his hands. The twin globes of solid, muscular flesh felt incredible as he squeezed and stroked, and Evan arched his butt into the pressure of Mark's caresses. As great as this was, Mark's straining cock was totally uncomfortable, trapped inside his briefs. He shifted slightly to the side and Evan broke the kiss then jumped to his feet. He grabbed

Mark's arm and hauled him off the couch. Face to face, Mark's body still tingling from Evan's touch and kisses, Evan feverishly began unbuttoning Mark's shirt. Mark tried to help but his fingers wouldn't cooperate and they ended up both yanking it over Mark's head. Evan's shirt followed, then they were chest to chest, bare skin sliding over bare skin, and Mark thought he might just swoon from the wonderful sensuous feeling.

Their mouths met again, this time more forcefully, verging on brutal. Bruised and swollen lips were definitely in both their futures. Evan fumbled with Mark's belt and his zipper, then he fell to his knees, taking Mark's jeans and briefs down with him.

"Oh, yeah..."

Mark's cock sprang out at him and he wasted no time, gripping it at the base and swirling his tongue over the glistening head. More sounds of approval came from deep in his throat as he scooped up the beads of pre-cum leaking from the slit. Mark gasped and arched his hips into the pull of Evan's sucking. He put his hands on either side of Evan's face, caressing the slightly bristly skin then running his fingers through the thick blond hair that crowned Evan's head.

Evan gazed up at him, his gray eyes darkened with lust, and Mark tensed, so near the edge when he looked back into those eyes and the sight of his cock sliding in and out between those lush, full lips.

"Evan, I don't want to come this quick..."

Evan stood and kissed him, his own impressive cock sticking out through his fly, at full mast. "You're right. I want to make this last. You're too gorgeous to rush it." He took Mark's cock in hand and slid it over his own. The friction made Mark see stars and he groaned.

"Come on," Evan whispered. "Step out of those jeans. My bed's better than the couch or the floor."

He slipped an arm around Mark's waist to steady him while he kicked off his shoes and jeans then led him into the bedroom. Evan shucked off his own jeans while Mark sat on the edge of the bed. No briefs, Mark noticed…commando. He liked that. He reached for Evan's cock then held it lightly in the palm of his hand. It was a thing of beauty. Long and thick with an upward curve. He shivered at the erotic thought of it sliding into him, something he hadn't wanted in a long time. It would hurt, without a doubt, yet deep inside, a part of him craved it. At the same time, he wondered how many men had salivated over watching Evan use it to its full advantage in his movies. Instead of finding that distasteful, he found himself growing even harder at the thought of Evan in action.

Mark looked up to take in the total visual that was Evan Ericson. Was there a part of him that was not perfection? Mark certainly couldn't find anything as his gaze flitted across Evan's wide shoulders, his muscled chest, each pectoral nicely defined, his nipples small and already hard, as if they were waiting for Mark to feast on them. He put a hand against Evan's torso and stroked the ridges of his abs. Evan, the perfect model, every gay man's wet dream. Amazing—and what was even more amazing, he was all Mark's right then.

"Mark…" Evan was gazing at him intently. "Just so you know, because of my…uh, past, I've been tested several times and thankfully, I'm clean. Don't want you to be nervous about getting this close to me."

"I appreciate you telling me." Mark didn't add he hadn't even considered that might be a problem. *Man, you are stupid. Thank God Evan is a lot more savvy than you…*

He leaned in and kissed Evan's cockhead, running the tip of his tongue over the swollen flesh, tasting him, inhaling his musky scent. He slipped a hand between Evan's legs to fondle his balls, squeezing gently, feeling them pull up tight under his caresses. Evan sucked in a breath then bent to kiss Mark, pushed him down on the bed and climbed on top of him. Now they were skin to skin, lips to lips, cock to cock, their bodies grinding together in a slow, rhythmic dance, the prelude to what Mark knew he desired more than anything else at that moment.

Evan was all over him, sucking on his lips, his ears, the hollow beneath his throat before moving down to take each nipple in his mouth, one at a time, licking and nibbling and driving Mark out of his mind with want and need. His body bucked as Evan trailed his mouth down over Mark's torso, dipping his tongue into Mark's navel, making him writhe with anticipation as Evan's stubbled cheek grazed Mark's cock. When Evan's lips encircled the head of Mark's painfully throbbing shaft, Mark thought he might just explode. He gritted his teeth and exerted all his willpower to not come in Evan's mouth, but the guy wasn't making it easy. He tugged at Evan's shoulders, hoping he'd get the message. Evan released him and looked up, mischief in his expression.

He swung his body around so that his dick was a tantalizing inch or so from Mark's mouth, then he rolled Mark onto his side and resumed his expert sucking. Mark didn't hesitate. He gripped Evan's erection at its base then ran his tongue up the hot length before devouring the head, taking it all the way to the back of his throat. He heard Evan gasp and liked the sound. It meant Evan was enjoying this too, although he could tell that already from the hard-as-steel cock pulsing in his mouth, and Mark relished each and every glorious inch of it.

He slid his lips up and down over the hard, throbbing length while he caressed and teased Evan's balls, bringing muffled groans of pleasure from him. Evan stroked Mark's butt, squeezing the twin globes of round, smooth flesh, dipping into the cleft and probing at Mark's opening. Mark's breath caught in his throat as Evan slid a finger inside him. His cock jumped when Evan found and stroked his sweet spot, sending lightning tingles pulsing through his blood. His balls tightened, ready to bring him to climax. He moaned and sucked harder, urging Evan on. He cupped Evan's muscular ass and pulled him deeper into his mouth.

He felt Evan's body stiffen and spasm, then Mark gulped and he almost choked on the torrent of hot, salty cream that filled his mouth. He threw his arms around Evan's waist, holding him until the spasms subsided. His own orgasm churned in his balls, the effect of Evan's strong sucking taking him over the edge. Lightning flashed behind his closed eyes and he came in great, body-shuddering jolts that he thought would never end, that he wished would never end. Evan gasped and Mark started to pull back but he was locked firmly in place by strong arms that encircled his body and held him fast. They lay quietly for a few moments, letting their breathing return to normal. Mark was content to stay, his face buried in Evan's groin, inhaling the scent of his pure, masculine musk.

Eventually, Evan scooted back to his original position and kissed Mark's lips with a tenderness that both surprised and thrilled Mark. Evan tightened his arms around Mark and nuzzled his throat, licking Mark's Adam's apple then sucking lightly on it.

"You'll get me going again if you keep that up."

"That's my intention," Evan murmured, gazing into Mark's eyes with mischievous intent. "I want to fuck you. Will you let me?"

"Maybe."

"Maybe?"

"Can I tell you something?"

"Of course."

"The last time I let someone fuck me, it was Corey, and he was not...uh, good at it. We'd done it a couple of times before, but this time...well, he was even more manic than usual. There was a kind of desperation there, I guess. He was way too eager, too rough. He kinda tore me..."

Evan stroked the hair off Mark's forehead. "Shit, I'm sorry."

"I'm not saying being fucked by you would be anything like that, but..."

"It's okay, Mark. The last thing I'd want to do is hurt you, or even come close to hurting you. Let's forget it for now. I kinda like just lying here, holding you, if that's okay."

Mark bit his lip. He felt as if he was letting Evan down, and he really didn't want to do that. He'd known that if he ever got this far with a man again the subject of 'going all the way' would come up, and he'd dreaded the thought of it. The memory of that last time with Corey was still enough to make him shudder and cause his sphincter muscles to clench involuntarily. But Corey was a thoughtless son of a bitch, and Evan... Well, he didn't know enough about Evan yet, didn't know him at all really, but he sensed there would be no comparison between the two men. Evan had already shown himself to be almost the opposite of Corey, the only resemblance being the fact they both had blond hair. And he had wondered how it would feel to have Evan inside him...

He stroked Evan's chest, teasing both nipples gently, making Evan shiver and press his hard-again cock against Mark's thigh.

"Okay," Mark murmured. "I want you to fuck me."

Evan moved and lay over Mark, gazing intently into his eyes. Mark could see his own reflection in the depths of those silver-gray orbs, and thankfully, he didn't look like a deer caught in the headlights.

"You sure? Absolutely, positively certain?"

Mark nodded as much as he could in their present position. He didn't want to kill the moment by banging his head on Evan's. "Yeah, I'm sure. Just go slow."

"I can do that."

He trailed his lips over Mark's mouth, nudging it open then giving him only the tip of his tongue. Mark sucked on it greedily then gasped when it tangled with his. The sensation was as if every nerve ending leading to his brain was being zapped. *Who the hell else can kiss like this?* Not that he had anyone to compare him with. *You spend two years hanging on to a guy who would never dream of kissing you, and that's what you get – nothing.* But this – this was Heaven on wheels. Mark groaned and pushed his erection into the heat of Evan's groin.

He writhed under Evan as the man scoured Mark's torso with his lips and tongue. He left a tingling trail on Mark's skin and had him moaning in ecstasy. He arched his body into the thrill of having Evan take him into his mouth, swallowing him to the root. Evan's tongue swirling up and down the length of Mark's rigid shaft was once more taking Mark to the brink. He delved his fingers into Evan's thick blond hair, tugging slightly, trying to warn him that he had to lessen this exquisite torture.

"Evan," he moaned, his eyes rolling back.

Evan released him slowly. He hooked Mark's legs over his shoulders then leaned down and pushed his face between Mark's butt cheeks, licking and sucking at Mark's opening.

Oh, dear God… No one had ever done this to him before. He almost laughed at the idea that Corey would even consider this for one fleeting nanosecond. His body bucked from the excruciating pleasure of Evan's tongue in his ass. He lifted his hips, giving Evan more access, writhing uncontrollably at the power of this incredible feeling that was enough to bring him to the point of no return. The heat that Evan's tongue created as he probed hard, the raw, primal instinct that had Mark pushing his ass into this amazing sensation, had him almost sobbing with need. Evan pulled back and Mark groaned his disappointment at the loss of that wet heat, but his heart leaped at the sight of Evan's beautiful body kneeling between his thighs. He watched, knowing his eyes must reflect a weird combination of anxiety and lust, when Evan rolled a condom over what looked to Mark like the hardest cock he had ever seen.

"Gonna get you ready," Evan whispered, spreading lube over his fingers. He circled Mark's hole with the cool gel then pushed in, first one finger, then two. Mark was not a virgin, but the memory of his last experience with Corey made him clench involuntarily against the invasion. "Easy," Evan murmured, "breathe and let me in…"

Evan took Mark's lips in yet another kiss that threatened to melt Mark's brain cells. He drew in a deep breath as the head of Evan's cock nudged at his opening. He lifted his legs again, wrapped them around Evan's waist and grasped him by the shoulders while Evan pushed forward. His body stiffened and he expelled the breath he was holding in a gasp of pain as Evan penetrated him.

Oh, Jesus…it hurts. He closed his eyes and bit down hard on his lower lip, trying to cover one kind of pain with another. Evan kissed Mark's face, his forehead, peppered his jaw with more kisses, crooned words Mark couldn't quite hear or understand, but he knew they were meant to soothe him. He opened his eyes and his heart lurched on seeing Evan's expression of tenderness and caring. Evan had paused, wasn't moving at all, and Mark mentally berated himself for being such a terrible fuck. Evan was doing everything he could to make this as enjoyable as possible. He had to pull himself together or this would end poorly for both of them.

"Evan," he murmured.

Lifting his hips, he drove himself onto Evan's shaft. It hurt like a son of a bitch but when Evan slid inside him, he drew in another breath, sharper this time. He couldn't ignore the burning sensation Evan's cock left in its wake, but as Evan went deeper and grazed Mark's prostate, a jolt of pleasure radiated through him, slightly diminishing the burn. He wound his arms around Evan's neck and dragged him down so he could take Evan's lips in a long, searing kiss. The visceral thrill eclipsed the discomfort entirely. They breathed into each other's mouths, sucking on each other's tongues. Mark stroked and caressed the sides of Evan's muscular torso then ran his hands down the smooth length of Evan's spine to cup his ass and pull him in even deeper.

Now fully seated inside Mark, Evan moved rhythmically over him, driving himself into Mark's core, his thrusts becoming stronger, more demanding. Mark keened his pleasure, arching his body up to meet Evan's as he slammed into him, each of his downward strokes igniting feelings within Mark he had never known before. This was real, primal and raw, unfettered passion, and this incredible man he held in his arms was the source, drawing out of Mark emotions he'd thought he would never be capable of again. Evan pushed a hand between their sweat-slicked torsos and grasped Mark's pulsing erection then pumped it rapidly, continuing to ram into him, Mark clinging to him, kissing him, matching his quickening pace. Evan let out a long, shuddering moan. His body stiffened in Mark's arms then spasmed, and he emptied himself into the condom buried deep inside Mark.

"*Mark...*" Evan's cry of ecstasy was muffled as he pressed his face into the moist warmth of Mark's neck. Mark arched under him, his orgasm ripping through him with a dizzying force that almost made him pass out. His cum sprayed across both their chests and one side of Evan's face. They lay panting in each other's arms, and Mark drew in a deep breath while he waited for the world to stop its crazy spinning. He sighed when Evan collapsed over him, whispering something that sounded like, "That was fucking amazing."

He wanted to agree but found he was too dazed to say anything at all.

* * * *

Some time passed while they lay wrapped in each other's arms, lost in their own thoughts, Mark enjoying, as he hoped Evan was too, the sweet euphoria of after-sex bliss. He'd never had this with Corey. Corey hadn't cuddled. Corey hadn't kissed or whispered sexy things in his ear. Corey had never made him laugh or feel good about himself.

Evan couldn't be more different in so many ways, which might be a bit of an unfair comparison as he really didn't know that much about the man apart from the fact he was beautiful and a hot lover, and if Mark's instincts were maybe correct, a nice guy.

He had been so sweet and caring about not wanting to hurt him, and Mark still couldn't quite believe that it had been so incredible after the initial pain. Pain, Mark now thought, that had been brought on partially because of his own fear that it might hurt as much as Corey had hurt him with his uncaring, clumsy attempt to dominate him.

A poke in the ribs brought him out of his ruminations. "Whatcha thinking about so hard?" Evan asked.

"You, and how much you've helped me get over this phobia I've had for such a long time."

"You mean about being…uh, what we just did?"

Mark chuckled. "Being fucked. Yeah, that."

"I was trying to avoid wounding your sensibilities," Evan huffed then grinned at him.

"Well, I appreciate that, and I just want to say I'm glad we met. I've really enjoyed spending time with you."

"And it's not over yet." He grabbed Mark's hand and pulled. "Let's go shower then I'll make us something to eat. Howzat?"

Mark loved Evan's energy even at—he glanced at the bedside clock—eleven-thirty. He let himself be tugged along behind Evan and, as usual, enjoyed the view. The man's butt really was a work of art. Like Michelangelo's David, the guy had buns of steel—and a cock that would make David weep with envy. Once inside the shower and under the hot spray, Evan rubbed body shampoo over Mark's chest while he nibbled on Mark's chin.

"Raise your arms."

Mark did as ordered and Even soaped up his armpits then slid his hands around and down Mark's spine before slipping his soapy fingers into Mark's crack.

"Oh yeah…" Evan breathed into Mark's ear. "Sweet butt. I love it."

"Love yours more," Mark murmured and pressed his lips to Evan's neck.

"You want it?"

"More than life." Mark chuckled. "Sorry, that was a bit over the top."

"I might let you over this top." Evan flashed him a wicked grin. "I pride myself on being versatile."

"Good to know."

Evan reached around to cup Mark's ass and finger his hole. Mark pushed back into Evan's probing and wriggled his hips to ease Evan's way inside. He took Mark's cock and his own in his free hand and slowly pumped them together side by side while he teased Mark's lips with his tongue. Evan added another finger, sliding deeper, finding Mark's prostate. Mark gasped and moaned low in his throat.

"Forget being versatile tonight," he murmured. "You're gonna have to fuck me, again—and I mean right now."

Chapter Four

Evan woke with the unfamiliar realization he wasn't alone in his bed. A lightly tan, leanly muscular arm was slung across his chest and a stubbly chin was pressed into his neck. *Ah, yes. Mark.* The guy he'd spent most of last night and a good part of the morning having sex with. And he'd asked him to stay the night. Not the first time he'd had a guy stay over, but it had been a long while since the last one. He usually preferred going back to whomever-he-was-going-to-fuck's place so that if things went south, or if he lost interest, he could get up and leave.

That was the trouble with having been in the porn industry — for him at any rate. He'd fucked so many guys that the excitement had worn off. The prospect of sex just didn't hold that same allure it once had. He was definitely jaded. He'd begun to think he could go for a long stretch without any sex at all. Until he'd met this guy, Mark. And wasn't that peculiar? Mark was hot, gorgeous really, but so were a lot of guys in LA and in the circles he moved in. So, what was it about Mark that set him apart from the others? For the life of him, Evan couldn't pinpoint just one thing — except maybe he was way nicer than most men he'd come across in the past several years. He frowned when he remembered how nervous and tentative Mark had been about getting fucked. What a jerk that Corey guy must have been to have hurt Mark so badly. No way was he good enough for Mark, or anybody else for that matter. Guys like that didn't really deserve someone as sweet as Mark.

Mark wasn't a total rarity. There were other nice guys out there, but over the years Evan had seen his share of jerks in Evan's life. They were the reasons why he'd never really looked for any kind of lasting sexual relationship. Admittedly, the kind of guys he mingled with—models, designers, actors, porn stars—were generally not the sweetest. There were exceptions, of course, but a great number of them had egos as big as Mount Shasta and it was just too much hard work to climb up and see what really went on at the top of the mountain. He'd become tired of the snark and constant one-upmanship that prevailed in the industries.

Breaking into mainstream movies was most likely not going to change very much of that—he'd still be dealing with egos, after all. But, God, he wanted this. Wanted the recognition that he wasn't just a pretty face, that he really could act, could hold his own along with the guys who had made it to the top of the heap.

A gentle snore from Mark made him smile. He stroked the young man's dark hair gently and kissed his forehead. "Time to wake up, sleepyhead," he whispered in Mark's ear. And it really was. Richard Harley wanted Mark for a screen test at ten, so he'd have to be looking his best, not as if he'd just fallen out of bed. Mark stirred and stretched his body alongside Evan's, rubbing his morning wood against Evan's thigh.

"Oh yeah?" Evan grinned at him. "Not had enough yet?"

Mark gazed at him dreamily. "I don't think I could ever get enough of you."

"You slept good. Maybe I exorcised Broken Nose from your dreams."

Mark yawned. "I think you did. Didn't think about him once." He kissed Evan on the mouth. "Thank you."

"Thank *you*. Now, I don't want to sound like I'm nagging, but you have a screen test this morning and you have to be all shiny and new, so…"

"Yikes!" Mark sat up straight. "You're right. I better head home, shower and pick out something to wear. First, I have to pee!" He rolled off the bed and ran for the bathroom.

Ruefully, Evan watched him go. He could have made good use of that lovely ass if they'd had more time. He got up and padded through to the kitchen to turn on the coffeemaker. Least he could do was give him a cup of java to go. While he waited for the coffee to brew he gazed out of the window at the verdant stretch of trees and grass in the park, which was now mostly empty, apart from one or two people walking their dogs in the early morning sunshine. An air of tranquility hung over the scene, so different from the mad rush of traffic on the other side of the building. He loved this view, even though it reminded him sometimes of where he used to live. Not home. He could never think of the house where he and his foster parents had lived as home...

The sound of Mark coming out of the bedroom jerked him from his thoughts and he turned to smile at Mark's disheveled appearance as he hurried into the kitchen, tucking his shirt inside his jeans. His thick dark hair stuck up at different angles where he'd obviously run damp hands through it in an unsuccessful effort to rid himself of bedhead. *He is...fucking adorable.*

"Made you some coffee. Take anything with it?"

"No, black is good, thanks." He looked at Evan shyly. "When will I see you again?"

Evan shrugged. "Soon as they start rehearsals, I expect."

"Oh." Mark appeared to be so downcast that Evan couldn't resist teasing him some more.

"That is, of course, if your screen test is a success."

Mark stared at him, his eyes wide. "Shit, I never even thought of that. What if I'm terrible? What if the director doesn't want me? Fuck!"

Evan laughed and put his arms around him. "Relax, you'll be great. I was just joshin'."

"Creep."

"Nerd."

"*Nerd?*" Mark stepped back in mock affront.

"Hot nerd, though." They laughed together, then Evan

handed him his to-go cup. "Good luck." He kissed Mark's lips lightly. "Knock 'em dead." He patted Mark's butt as he headed for the door.

He drank his coffee quickly, poured himself another cup then hurried into the bathroom. *Just enough time for a shower.*

* * * *

Woodside Studios was alive with voices and movement when Evan pushed the door open as quietly as he could. Richard Harley was conversing with two other men who he recognized as Charles Bennet, the director, and Roger King, the cameraman who'd been in charge of Evan's screen test. A couple of other men were moving lights into place. Pamela Fisher, the script coordinator, was talking to Mark while Connie Vaughn was applying some last-minute makeup touches to Mark's face.

They're nice. Most likely trying to put Mark at ease.

No one had seen him come in, which had been his intention. He wanted it to be a surprise, hopefully a good one, for Mark. His last night's lover looked good, he thought. His hair was still untidy, but artfully so under Connie's primping, no doubt. A couple of dark locks hung over his eyebrows and Evan's fingers itched to push them back then rumple them again. He felt himself grow hard. Mark really was a gorgeous guy. The loose-fitting white shirt and tight black jeans he wore enhanced his lean, elegant physique and posture.

The camera will love him…

"Okay, people…" Charles Bennet clapped his hands to gain attention. "We're ready for you, Mark, so please step over to where we've placed the easel and canvas. Richard tells me you've read this scene with Evan, so we'll use that for the first test, okay?"

Evan moved closer but kept out of everyone's sightline. He didn't want Mark to see him just yet. He listened as Richard Harley told Mark he would read the other character's—

Jeff's — lines. He waited until Mark was in place, the lights were positioned to Charles' liking and the word 'action' was given. Still staying in the shadows as much as he could, he walked up behind Harley. He needn't have worried. All eyes were riveted on Mark as he said the lines which he now obviously knew by heart.

"Just for the record, what is it about me that makes you think I had anything to do with blackmailing Samantha Goodall? I told you last time we talked that I barely knew the woman, now you're acting like I'm the only suspect. Let's get this straight once and for all, I did not blackmail her, nor did I kill her!"

Evan tapped Richard on the shoulder, and as surprise made the man hesitate, Evan stepped from behind him and said, "Has anyone ever told you you're kind of hot when you get all defensive?"

Mark registered only the slightest surprise. *Good man, you can take it in your stride.* Mark raised an eyebrow. "Detective, you are not scoring any brownie points with me using that type of approach. Apart from it being inappropriate, it's cheesy at best."

Evan moved into camera shot. "Cheesy, huh?" He laughed and started to undo the buttons on Mark's shirt. "I guess I'll have to improve my pick-up lines. How about this?" He ripped Mark's shirt open and pulled him into his arms. This time, Evan noticed Mark's mouth wasn't open from shock, just ready for the moment when he would kiss him. And again, Evan's tongue glided effortlessly between Mark's parted lips.

"Cut!" Charles strode forward. "What the hell, Evan?"

His arms still around Mark, Evan grinned at him. "You didn't like it?"

"Yes, I liked it, but a little warning would've been good." He turned to Roger. "Did you get it all, or did you stop rolling when our maverick here decided to get in on the action?"

"I got it all," Roger assured him. "You're gonna want to

see it."

As Charles walked away, Evan kissed Mark's cheek and murmured, "You didn't mind, did you?"

"Mind? I loved it." He gave Evan a mischievous smile. "We might even get to do it again."

"Over and over, as many times as you want."

"Okay, you two lovebirds," Charles yelled. "Get over here and look at this." They walked over to where a group had gathered round the camera monitor. The initial image of Mark standing by the easel brought a murmur of appreciation from Connie and Pamela, and one of the crew whispered, "Hot." Mark's dialog was clear and crisp and just slightly annoyed. *Perfect.* The chemistry between himself and Mark was palpable during their scene together, so much so that the group applauded at the end of the scene.

"Well..." Charles smiled as he looked at them both. "I think we have Peter Jennings, our artist." He rubbed his hands together with satisfaction. "And we can start rehearsals on schedule. Mark, I'll need you for some more camera angles, if Evan can leave you alone for an hour or two?"

"Reluctantly, I can," Evan said cheekily, resulting in titters from the crew.

Richard clapped them both on the shoulders. "I told Charles how well you did yesterday. I don't think any of the reviews are going to complain about the way you two react to each other. The chemistry's already there. Excellent, guys. Thank you."

* * * *

Evan headed for the restroom while the crew set up for Mark's camera angles. His cell chimed as he was washing his hands. Drying off quickly, he checked the ID screen. *Dareck...*

"Hey," he said, trying to sound unsurprised.

"Dean, how are you?" Dareck's Hungarian accent was

unmistakable.

"Good. What's up?"

"I have trouble, my friend."

Uh-oh. Trouble is this guy's middle name. "What d'you mean?"

"I need money. Can you help me?"

"How much?"

"Two thousan' dollar."

"Wow. What happened?"

"I have to leave America—go back home, real soon. Can you help me? I need to know right way, otherwise must hide."

"Hide? What the hell did you do?" Whatever it was wouldn't be much of a shock. Dareck's behavior had always had a propensity to be off the charts, especially when he was under the influence.

"I borrow money from these guys for…you know…what I need. I can't pay back. They say they cut off my dick if I don' pay. I need my dick, Dean."

Evan bit down the urge to laugh. Yeah, Dareck's dick was all the talent he had. A good-looking guy but dumb as a rock. He'd been fired from so many studios for showing up stoned and unable to get hard for the scenes he was hired to shoot. He'd also gotten into trouble trying to blackmail a guy he'd lived with for a short time. It had been all over the tabloids, Dareck saved from a jail sentence only because the guy hadn't pressed charges. Evan doubted that Dareck had thought of the blackmail plot himself. He honestly believed Dareck just didn't have that kind of deviousness in his body, but he most certainly could be led by the nose to go through with it. Whoever had persuaded him to do it had done him no favors.

He hadn't seen Dareck in months, hadn't really wanted to since he'd given up on the porn industry. The guy still thought of him as 'Dean'. But he couldn't just look the other way and let him get hurt. They might not cut off his dick, but drug dealers had nasty ways of meting out punishment when they got stiffed. He'd seen a couple of their victims when he'd been involved with drugs himself, and it hadn't been pretty. It was nice to reflect that one time he'd managed to exact some revenge on a couple of the bastards...but that was then, and no longer a part of his life.

"Dean, you still there? I need your help, please."

Evan sighed. "Okay. How soon do you need the money?"

"Today! I want to book fare so I can leave soon as I can."

Shit. That meant he'd have to go to the bank and meet Dareck right away. He'd wanted to stay for Mark's screenshots then take him to lunch to celebrate. *Damn...*

"Where will I meet you?"

"Oh, Dean, thank you. I will say prayers for you every night for the rest of my life. I am at Jet's on Melrose. I will stay here till you come. It's always busy here, so it's safe."

"Okay, I should be there in about an hour or so."

"You are my savior, Dean!"

"Bye, Dareck." Evan ended the call and cursed under his breath. Apart from this fucking up his and Mark's day, he really couldn't afford to hand over two grand that he had no possibility of ever getting back. Once Dareck was in Hungary, he'd most likely never hear from him again. But at least he'd have a clear conscience about not letting the guy get beaten up, or worse. Thank God, his paycheck from the movie would start this week. His dwindling savings account was going to take a severe hit from this latest bite at the balance.

He trailed back to where Mark was getting ready to face the camera again. "Hey, Mark. Sorry, I wanted to stay but I got a call and a friend needs to see me, so I'll be in touch later, okay?"

Mark looked disappointed but nodded in understanding. "That's okay, sure. And thanks for being here. It was great to know how it's gonna feel working with you." He gave Evan a tentative smile. "See you later, then?"

"Yeah, later." Evan turned away and walked quickly to the exit. Now that the full effect of Dareck's call was sinking in, he had a bad feeling in the pit of his stomach. After a year plus of being out of the porn industry and more or less distancing himself from anyone he'd known during that time, it was disconcerting at how easily memories came flooding back — most of them bad.

Dareck had been one of his first partners on film. Sweet-faced, with long blond hair that hung to his shoulders and had to be constantly swept out of his eyes, there was a naïveté about him that had made Evan feel protective toward him in the beginning. Trade naïveté for sheer stupidity and that was Dareck. Evan couldn't quite believe the dumb things the kid would get into. *Kid…* He was only three years younger than Evan but made decisions a twelve year old would think were stupid. Constantly stoned, he soon became useless on set as he couldn't perform and had, on occasion, passed out under the guy fucking him. He would end up in Evan's apartment sobbing his heart out over getting fired and swearing he'd never touch another drug. That would last perhaps a couple of days, then he'd end up in the hospital or in a police cell or back in Evan's apartment, high as a kite.

Maybe the best thing for him was to return to his homeland. Evan thought he still had parents there, and he was young enough to go back to school and start over — if he could keep away from drugs. *Whatever.* Los Angeles and the porn studios, where the products of his addiction were so readily available, were obviously the worst factors in Dareck's life. And wasn't it sad that the only one Dareck felt he could turn to was Dean Masters? They hadn't been in touch for close to a year. Dareck didn't even know his real name, and yet there was no one else he was close enough to that he could ask for help. Or maybe he had and they'd turned him down. *Poor kid.*

Compared to some of the other guys he'd worked with, Dareck was an angel — a fallen angel maybe — but not someone who'd go out of their way to injure anyone, not even their feelings. And there were a few who would do just that. The bitchiness that had pervaded the atmosphere of some of the scenes he'd done still made him cringe when he thought about it. He'd only reacted once to a slur he'd overheard cast his way. Something he didn't regret, even though it had been the catalyst that had ended his career. He'd wanted out, but at the time he'd felt right about taking a stand against being bad-mouthed — especially by a guy he was supposed to fuck that morning.

"No way," he'd told the producer while trying to maintain a calm but firm attitude. "If you think for one minute I'm letting him put that filthy mouth anywhere near me then you're nuts and I'm through." There hadn't been another 'model' to take the creep's place, and no amount of persuasion or half-hearted apologies from the producer had deterred him from leaving — and that had been the end of his porn career.

* * * *

After drawing out the cash at the bank he drove over to Melrose and parked behind Jet's Café. Dareck was sitting at the back in a corner. He was a mess. His once golden hair was lank and dirty, his face pale and drawn, his eyes red and puffy. It was as if he'd been on a bender for a week.

"Hey, Dareck." Evan forced a smile to his lips as he gazed down at the young man. Evan had to remind himself Dareck was only twenty-three. From his appearance, he could have been ten years older.

"Dean!" Dareck sprang to his feet and threw his arms around Evan. "Oh, I am so glad to see you…so glad." Tears dampened the front of Evan's shirt and he pushed him gently back into his seat. He sat opposite him, doing his best to hide the sadness, and yes, some of the anger he felt at such a waste of a life.

This could've been me if I hadn't pulled myself together and quit the drugs and the sex games.

"Dareck..." Evan kept his voice low and gentle. "What happened to you? You don't look well."

Dareck nodded. "I am sick, Dean. Very sick. I have HIV. I must go home. My mother will take care of me. I wrote, but she has no money to send me, but she said if I come home, she will take care me." The tears fell freely now and Evan handed him some table napkins to wipe his face. "Can you drive me to the airport, please, Dean?"

Evan wondered if they would let him fly looking as bad as he did. "Do you have medications?"

"Yes. Not a lot, but I will see doctor in Budapest. Did you bring money, Dean?"

Evan handed him the envelope the bank cashier had put the money in. "Don't buy any drugs, Dareck. Promise me you won't."

"I promise. The drugs are killing me, the doctor said. Infected needle. I think I will die soon, Dean, but I will be home."

"Dareck." Evan took his hand. "Don't talk like that. HIV can be controlled these days. Just make sure you get a good doctor over there. Did you call the airline about plane times?"

"Yes, there is one on Czech airlines at four. Is expensive because last minute, but I cannot wait. If they find me..."

"Right. Finish your coffee and we can leave for LAX."

* * * *

On the way to the airport, Dareck kept up an ongoing tirade about how badly he'd been treated by so many people. Evan kept quiet and let him rant. There wasn't really much point in telling him most of this was his own fault. He didn't need to hear Evan talk about his bad decisions and poor judgment when it came to the basic things in life. Dareck was just another in a long line of people who saw themselves as victims. In a way, he was, and Evan wished now that he had been more of a friend to him. He thought of how many other guys he'd worked with in the porn industry who might be in similar situations. It was so fucking depressing!

There was a problem at the ticket counter because Dareck's work visa had long expired and the airline agent didn't want to issue him a ticket. Evan asked to see her supervisor and she suddenly capitulated after a long look at Dareck's Hungarian passport. Evan wondered at that but said nothing. Maybe she'd been in trouble earlier and didn't want to call the supervisor again. Or she'd figured the officials in Hungary could deal with it. Whatever, Dareck had his ticket and Evan walked with him as far as security. Once there, Dareck threw his arms around Evan again and kissed him, his slim body trembling with emotion and fatigue in Evan's arms.

Evan had to fight back his own tears as he watched Dareck pass through the security check. He breathed a sigh of relief when Dareck was cleared and allowed to proceed toward the departure gate. Dareck stopped to wave at him, his body language one of complete despondency. Evan waved back and gave him an encouraging smile and a thumbs-up. Sighing, Evan turned away and walked quickly through the terminal to where he'd parked his car.

He called Mark on the way, smiling when he heard Mark's cheerful, "Hi!"

"How'd the test go?" he asked.

"Good. They seem pleased with everything. Where are you?"

"At LAX. It's a long story. I'll tell you later when I see you. Are you at home?"

"Yeah. I'd ask you over, but my roommates will be back soon…"

"Come over to my place and I'll take you out for dinner. We need to celebrate our working together."

"Sounds great. I am so thrilled about that, Evan. You have no idea."

"Me too. I'll show you how much when I see you. I should

be home, traffic willing, about five. Okay?"

"See you then!"

Chapter Five

Mark was just stepping out of the bathroom he shared with his roommates when he heard Andrew sing out, "Anybody home?"

"Not just anybody," Mark replied.

"Oh, hi, Mark." Andrew's gaze swept over Mark's damp-from-the-shower body and he licked his lips. "There's a sight for sore eyes." He chuckled as Mark shifted uncomfortably. "Just jesting. So, how'd it go yesterday? We did notice you didn't come home last night," he added with a knowing smile.

"Let me put some shorts on and I'll fill you in," Mark said, hurrying into his room. *Better put on a tee as well, or Andrew will be licking his lips again.* He liked Andrew, but the guy wasn't at all subtle about leering at just about any dude's body. When he went into the living room, Andrew was making coffee.

"Like some?"

"That'd be great."

"So, it's tell-all time," Andrew sing-songed. He did that a lot. Mark had thought it cute when they'd first met, but it had gotten kind of old after a while.

"Okay, I got the part in the movie."

"You did?" Andrew screamed and caught Mark up in a bone-crushing bear hug. *For a skinny guy he sure is strong... ouch!* "That's fantastic, Mark. I am so happy for you. Omigod, wait 'til Perry hears about this. He will be soooo jealous!"

Mark had no doubt of that, but he was glad Andrew sounded sincere. "Yeah, it's exciting," he said, extricating himself from Andrew's hug.

"So, what's it called? Who's in it? Who's the director? Come on, spill. Enquiring minds want to know!"

Mark laughed and was about to reply when the front door opened and Perry walked in. He looked at Mark, then at Andrew's excited expression, then back at Mark, eyebrows raised.

"*Now* what's going on?"

"Mark got that part in the movie he auditioned for yesterday. Isn't that a kick in the pants?"

Perry frowned at Andrew then turned to Mark and held out his hand. "That is good news indeed, Mark. I hope it is a huge success for you."

Andrew rolled his eyes. "You could be a little more enthusiastic, Per. Give him a hug, for goodness' sake."

"I'll leave all the sappy over-emotional shit for you," Perry said dryly. "And don't call me *Per*. You know I hate it."

"And of course it's all about you, as usual." Andrew didn't even try to hide his disdain. "Well, I think it's fantastic. We have a movie star for a roommate!"

Mark chuckled. "Not quite."

"Anyway," Andrew gushed, "you were about to tell me all about it before old killjoy walked in."

"I am not a killjoy, and I too want to hear all about it," Perry said, sitting on the couch. "Is that coffee I smell? Thank you, Andy, I'll have a cup."

"*Honestly.*" Andrew stomped into the kitchen, and Mark grinned at the sound of cups being banged about.

Perry gazed at him, his expression impassive. "I really am very pleased for you, Mark, even if our eccentric roomie thinks otherwise. It's an indie movie, you said?"

Mark nodded. "Yeah. A Light in the Forest production. One of the producers, Richard Harley, actually wrote the script. It's pretty good, I think."

"What's it about?" Andrew bustled out carrying a tray holding three mugs of steaming coffee.

"A murder mystery set in the fifties. I play an up-and-coming artist who is suspected of murder. The detective on the case and the artist become involved sexually."

"How fabulous!" Andrew presented the tray to Perry and curtsied as he did so.

"Stop that nonsense," Perry growled. "So who else is in it?"

"Well, the actor playing the detective is Evan Ericson. I hadn't heard of him, but we did a scene together yesterday and he's really good."

"Evan Ericson…" Andrew looked thoughtful. "That name rings a bell. I think I just read something about him. Wait, it was in *Screen* magazine the other day. I'll just go get it."

"He reads all that crap," Perry said, not too dismissively. "Ask him what any celebrity, minor or major, is doing, who they're doing, who's getting divorced, all that shit, and he's got the answer right there." He shook his head. "He is a fount of useless information."

Mark chuckled as Andrew came bouncing back into the room. "Here it is," he exclaimed, shoving the magazine at Mark. "Evan Ericson signed to appear in new indie movie *Burning Hearts!*"

"Ericson is relatively unknown…" Mark continued to read at Andrew's prompting, "but that will change fast, says director Charles Bennet. 'Evan is already an accomplished actor and works seamlessly in front of the camera'.

"When asked about Ericson's past experience, Bennet was vague, but *Screen* has discovered that Ericson was once known as Dean Masters and has appeared in several porn movies. Looks like he's trying to break into the mainstream which, as we know, folks, ain't easy."

Mark sighed. "Well, shit."

"You didn't know?" Perry asked.

"Yes, I know. Richard Harley, the producer, was upfront about Evan's past career, but he's willing to give him the break he thinks he deserves. And he's really good, guys."

"Yeah, but that kind of notoriety is hard to make go

away," Perry said, frowning.

"What a shame." Andrew took his magazine back and stared at the picture of Evan. "He is a beauty, though. Maybe the critics will be so stunned they'll overlook that part of his life."

Perry snorted. "Maybe, but the scandal sheets won't. I hate to say it, Mark, but this could be the only legit movie he gets to make."

"Or the publicity will be controversial enough to make the movie a success," Andrew remarked. "That has happened before."

"Andrew," Perry snapped, "name me one gay porn star who has made it big in real movies. Go on – just one. I didn't think so," he added when Andrew came up with nothing.

"Well, the people at Light in the Forest Productions have faith in him," Mark said, "and just for the record, so do I. He can act, and he looks great, and he's a really nice guy... And I'm having dinner with him tonight, to celebrate my getting the part."

"That is so wonderful." Andrew gazed at him, a big smile on his face. "And so romantic!" He hugged Mark while Perry laughed quietly from his place on the couch.

"Andrew's right," Perry said. "And you should enjoy every minute of it." He didn't add, 'because it won't last' but the unspoken words hung heavily in the air regardless.

"Thanks, guys." Mark forced a smile to his lips. "I better get dressed. I'm meeting Evan at his place at five."

The look that passed between Andrew and Perry spoke volumes, without a word being said by either of them.

* * * *

Mark's heart skipped a beat when Evan opened the door to his apartment. He looked incredible as always, but right then the tight pale-blue jeans and silver-gray shirt he wore just seemed to enhance his natural beauty. The silver shirt matched his eyes to perfection... *Had he known that when he bought it?* And the jeans accentuated the muscular curves of his legs. Without seeing it, Mark knew Evan's ass would be spectacular encased in that tight denim.

"C'mere, sexy," Evan murmured as he pulled Mark into his arms and kicked the door closed behind them. The kiss he laid on Mark's eager mouth was enough to fry his brain. He pushed himself into the warmth of Evan's embrace, inhaling the clean scent of Evan's fresh-from-the-shower skin.

"I got us a bottle of champagne to celebrate," Evan said when they came up for air. He took Mark's hand and led him into the dining area. On the table was a bucket of ice holding a champagne bottle and glasses chilling. Evan popped the bottle like an expert sommelier and poured them a glass each of the bubbly. "Here's to us, Mark, and the success I know our movie will be."

Mark clinked his glass against Evan's and smiled. "Yeah, I'll drink to that." He tried to block from his mind the dark predictions his roommates had made, especially Perry's assertion that not one gay porn star had ever made it into the mainstream. Evan might yet prove to be the exception, and if it really was all about talent, then Evan had it in spades.

He leaned in and kissed Evan. "I can't wait till we start rehearsals. It's gonna be a blast working with you."

"Likewise." Evan took a sip of his champagne then pressed his lips to Mark's and let the bubbly flow into Mark's mouth. "Mmm… I saw that in a movie and thought it was really sexy."

"It is." Mark put his glass down on the table and wrapped his arms around Evan. "You gonna fuck me before we go out to dinner?"

"You must have read my mind." He also put his glass down and unbuttoned Mark's shirt. "You look good in blue — but even better out of it."

Evan slipped the shirt over Mark's shoulders then hung it

over the back of a chair. He nuzzled Mark's nipples, licking and nibbling them one at a time and driving himself crazy with lust. He was ready to pull Mark down onto the floor, but instead backed him into the bedroom and threw him on the bed.

"Want you," Mark murmured against Evan's mouth as they locked lips.

"Want you too…"

"You have a condom handy?"

"Want me that much, huh?" Evan teased him.

"You know I do, and it'll be easier this time. I mean, if you're careful again. You're big, but — "

Evan put a finger on Mark's lips to quieten him. "Don't worry, it's going to be even better this time around, and the next and the next."

Mark looked up at him with big eyes. "And the next?"

"And the next." Evan teased him with a fleeting kiss then ran his lips straight down Mark's torso, lifting his legs as he did so. He licked his way over Mark's cock and balls then went for the gold between Mark's ass cheeks. His eager pucker responded to Evan's insistent, probing tongue and Evan added a finger, sliding in to stroke and excite Mark's prostate. Keeping his finger there, he licked his way back up to Mark's balls, tugging gently and rolling each one between his lips before taking Mark's straining erection into his mouth.

The taste of Mark's pre-cum spilling generously onto his tongue inflamed Evan's senses, an aphrodisiac all by itself. The room was filled with the erotic sounds of Mark's moans and whimpers as Evan sucked him with a skill honed by a lot of practice. Even though he hadn't indulged very much since those days, until Mark, he hadn't forgotten how to pleasure a guy and bring him to the brink of orgasm as fast or as slowly as he wished. But there was nothing of the automaton in the way he made love to Mark. The bonus here was that he really, really enjoyed having sex with him and wanted him to love it as much as he did. From the sounds of things, he was achieving that goal.

He paused for a moment to reach for the lube and a condom. He wanted to be inside Mark so much he feared he might just come from the thought of it. *Jeez, when did I start having a problem with EE?* Well, it hadn't happened yet, but as he eased the condom over his aching dick, the look of lust on Mark's face was enough to trigger it. Hastily, he lubed Mark's hole then nudged it with the head of his cock. Mark lifted his hips in invitation, one that Evan was only too eager to accept, but he took care not to go in too fast.

"Okay?" he whispered.

"Yes." Mark caressed Evan's thighs and torso as Evan pushed in slowly. Mark's eyes flew open and he groaned, but he pulled Evan forward as if to tell him it was still okay. Evan stretched the muscles in his back and bent low so that he could take Mark's erection in his mouth.

"Oh, my God!" Mark's shock and surprise filled Evan with delight. *Another first for Mark*, he thought, loving the way Mark writhed and mewled in ecstasy. Evan pumped and sucked to an erotic rhythm, thrusting harder into Mark while he swirled his tongue up and down the length of Mark's pulsing cock. When Mark's breath began to rasp in his chest, Evan, with one long final suck, released him from his mouth but took him in hand, pumping Mark's rigid shaft to his own quickening rhythm.

He leaned down to take Mark's lips with a bruising kiss, letting him taste his own pre-cum, working his tongue into every corner of Mark's mouth, grinding their bodies together until Mark, with a muffled cry, came in jolting spasms under Evan, his cum surging between their torsos. Evan gasped at the ferocity of Mark's orgasm and found himself teetering on the edge of his own climax. Heat flooded his body, a shudder rippled down his spine and he cried out before he fell into a lightning-streaked blackness.

Evan collapsed over Mark and tightened his arms around his lover's lean, supple body. He nuzzled the hollow under Mark's throat and kissed his sweat-slicked skin.

"Okay?" he murmured.

"Absolutely," Mark replied. "Let's do it again."

* * * *

The restaurant Evan had chosen was just about perfect, in Mark's opinion. It was a small Italian ristorante on Santa Monica Boulevard. Evan knew the manager, a handsome man in his thirties, Ronaldo, who took them to a table for two in an intimate corner, then brought them a complimentary bottle of the house pinot noir.

"That's nice of you," Evan told Ronaldo, and they smiled at each other in a way that made Mark wonder if there was history between them. A pang of jealousy tugged at his heart and he had to look away from the very personal moment the men were sharing. *Come on, no way can Evan not have had close relationships with other men. Look at him… he's fucking gorgeous.* Mark's own self-esteem took a serious hit at that moment and he cursed himself for being stupid.

He's here with you, isn't he?

"Mark…" Evan was smiling into his eyes and Mark felt his brain turn to mush. Just basking in this gorgeous man's smile for the rest of his life might be enough. "*Mark.*"

"Yes, Evan…sorry."

"I wanted to propose another toast."

"Right." Mark glanced at the wine glass Evan was holding. He hadn't even noticed the wine being poured. He held his up and smiled when Evan said, "*Salud.*"

"*Salud,* and thank you for thinking of this. The place is really nice."

"It is, isn't it? I used to come here a lot during my modeling days. Ronaldo was a model too, a real pro. He was so good to me when I was a newbie. When he retired he bought this place as an investment. *He* was clever with his money. Anyway, again, to us, Mark, and to the future."

They sipped their wine. "Excellent," Mark said, appreciating the flavor and feeling better now that Evan had explained his closeness to Ronaldo. *You really need to get a grip, dickhead. It's way too early to be feeling jealous of anyone Evan knows. You met him yesterday, for Pete's sake...* But strangely, yesterday already seemed a long time ago.

"Sorry I missed the rest of your camera shots." Evan ran his fingertips over the back of Mark's hand as he spoke. "Did you sign the contract also?"

"Yes. I was a bit startled when I read the clause giving them permission to include frontal nudity. I guess I should have expected it when they told me there would be a nude love scene — with you." Mark blushed slightly.

"Yeah, lucky me." He grinned at Mark. "Anyway, like I said, sorry I wasn't there for moral support."

"Or immoral, as the case may be." Mark returned Evan's grin. "You said you had to go to the airport?"

"Yeah. A friend got himself into some trouble so I helped him out with a ride."

"What kind of trouble?"

"Money — and who he borrowed from."

"A good friend?"

"Not really. A kid I knew when we were both in porn." He didn't think Mark would want to hear about him fucking Dareck, even if it was just what he'd done for a living at the time. "Unfortunately, he's not the brightest bulb in the chandelier, and easily led astray. I feel guilty about not being a better friend to him at the time, but at least I was able to help him go back home where he'll be safe."

"He was in danger?"

Evan nodded. "Owed money to drug dealers. They don't like it when you can't pay them back."

"Where does he live?"

"Hungary."

"Oh, wow. Don't suppose they'll want to follow him that far."

"That's what he figured. Also, he said he's sick, Mark. HIV. His mother said she'd take care of him."

"Poor guy."

"Yeah, I hope it works out for him over there."

Ronaldo appeared at their table at that moment, with menus and a list of specials that kept them occupied for the next few minutes while they decided what to have.

"Did you tell your roomies about getting the part in *Burning Hearts*?" Evan asked once they'd put their order in.

"Yeah...they were excited at first, but—"

"But what? Were they mean to you?"

"Oh, not really." Mark seemed to hesitate and Evan took his hand and squeezed it gently.

"It was about me, wasn't it?"

"Kind of. Andrew showed me this piece in *Screen* about you having a past as a porn star. Of course, I told them I already knew, but they think it's a downer, that the movie won't be a success, that porn stars can't make the change to mainstream. That kind of junk."

Evan grimaced. "It isn't really junk. Charles and Richard know they are taking a chance on me, but they're the ones who want me to do it. They approached me with the offer. I have to admit, I was surprised when they did. It's almost like they want to prove that it's possible."

"And they're willing to gamble their movie and their money on you. I think that's terrific."

"Or terrifically stupid. Let's face it, Mark, this industry is as cutthroat as it gets. The critics will have a field day if I don't pull this off. And even if I do, the tabloids will love exposing me—and I do mean expose. There are enough nude pics of me out there to fill a whole magazine."

"I'd love to have that magazine," Mark said, making Evan laugh. "Maybe they're banking on the controversy to make people curious enough to fill the seats."

"That's what I think too. And if it works, then I'm fine with it." Evan grinned at him. "Even if it goes to HBO. Look at the success Showtime had with *Queer as Folk*. I never understood why they didn't make a movie to wrap things up better. But if any of the cable companies picks it up, we could be nominated for an Emmy. Think of that!"

Mark laughed. "Wouldn't that shake the naysayers up a little."

"I think we would rock their world."

"Well, you've certainly rocked mine," Mark said.

Evan gave him a seductive smile. "And I mean to do that again, and again…"

"You're making me hard, and here comes our food," Mark warned him. "Now I have to eat with an erection between my legs."

"Very hedonistic." Evan winked then leaned back in his seat as the waiter laid their plates in front of them. "I'll take care of that second issue after dinner."

Even though the waiter could have no idea what Evan was referring to, Mark blushed, much to Evan's amusement. He waited until the young man had left, then said, "I love that despite everything, you are still such an innocent."

"Who, me?" Mark bristled. "I'll have you know I'm very much a man of the world."

Evan chuckled. "Oh, you so are." He was glad Mark wasn't quite as worldly as his own past acquaintances in both the modeling business and, later, the porn industry. Any business that depended principally on a person's looks and ability to project some kind of allure on camera was ultra-competitive, and Evan would often be amazed at the lengths some of his fellow models would go to procure the often-elusive jobs.

"You've gone quiet," Mark said.

"Italian food always make me reminisce." As good an excuse as any, he thought.

"Really? About what?"

"I did a lot of work in Rome and Venice when I was modeling." Evan wound a small amount of fettuccini around his fork and lifted it to his mouth. His eyes met Mark's as he chewed slowly.

"God, you even make that look sexy," Mark said.

"Are you still hard?"

"Tease."

Evan smiled. "Are you enjoying the tagliatelle?"

"Yes, but tell me about when you were modeling in Italy, sounds exciting."

"It was. But several years of being feted and pampered can give you a slanted view of the world. You start to take it all for granted after a while. Like it's going to be your place in the world forever, or at least for the foreseeable future. You soak up the adulation, accept the gifts like you deserve them." He tapped his elegant watch for effect. "Then when it starts to fade — when the times between shoots become longer and your agent tells you 'sorry, nothing for you' — it's a harsh reality check."

"I still don't understand why that would happen to you, even because of the drugs," Mark said. "You cleaned yourself up, so why weren't they clamoring for you then?"

"Because there were a hundred new guys, all fresh-faced and willing to take over. I became yesterday's news." Evan shrugged. "It happens. I just wasn't prepared for it. Besides, there was the porn connection by then, and that's a big no-no in the fashion industry."

Mark grimaced. "Their loss."

"You are the sweetest guy." Evan leaned over the table and kissed Mark's cheek. "Good to have you on my side."

Mark was blushing again. "Sometimes when I look at you, I can't believe I'm going to be in a movie with you, never mind the fantastic sex we've shared. I think I'll wake up any minute and this will all have been a dream."

"No chance, kiddo. This is as real as it gets. And don't you think that I consider myself really lucky too? Meeting you has been one delight after another, in and out of bed. You are a special kind of guy, Mark." Evan chuckled. "You know I say things like that just so I can see you blush, don't you?"

"Creep."

"Nerd."

They burst out laughing together, then Evan said, "So, eat

up and drink up. I have major plans in mind for you when we get back to my apartment."

"You're insatiable."

"Damn straight. Ain't you the lucky one?"

"Damn straight I am."

* * * *

Just before they ordered dessert, Mark said, "You know, you've mentioned your modeling career, but what about before that? I don't even know where you were born and raised."

Evan grimaced. "Not something I talk a lot about…"

"Oh, sorry…if I'm being too nosy, just ignore the question."

"No, you're not being too nosy." Evan's smile seemed a tad off, but he took Mark's hand and squeezed it gently. "Hey, if we're gonna be friends, you should know stuff like that, I guess. I was born in San Mateo. Don't remember much about it, though. My mother wasn't married to my dad. In fact, I don't know who they were, Mark."

"Oh, shit…I am sorry…"

Evan shrugged. "That's not exactly true. I mean, I never knew them, but I do have a birth certificate that says my mother was Anne Ericson, and father unknown."

"So you were adopted?"

"Nope. I'll make this really short, because it's not something I like talking about, but you asked, so…"

"No, really…" Mark gripped Evan's hand tightly. "If it's painful, you don't have to relive it for me."

"It's okay. A lot of it I don't actually remember. Bits and pieces come back to me at times, but the first few years of my life are a haze. I was eventually fostered out to a couple who, I guess you'd laughingly call it, raised me. They were the ones who filled in the blanks. With great relish, they told me that my mother was a whore who couldn't say no to any guy, and I was the product of one of those lucky gents. Bert and Molly…" Evan paused and shuddered. "They were supposed to adopt me but never did. We lived outside of town. They had three other kids, one of their own and two fostered. It was miserable, I hated them — every one of them — and when I was twelve I ran away."

No need to tell him about the abuse…

Mark stared at him, his eyes wide. "You were only twelve?"

Evan nodded. "I made it as far as Redwood City, where I was picked up by the cops for wandering about the streets late at night. I refused to tell them where I'd come from 'cause I knew they'd only ship me back to dear old Bert and Molly. No way was that gonna happen. Told them I was an orphan and they handed me over to child care authorities. I guess Bert and Molly never reported me missing, which is kinda funny, as they'd lose money with me gone. Maybe they hated me as much as I hated them.

"Anyway, I was in an institution for homeless kids for four years. Actually, that wasn't as bad as it sounds — better than the foster home. I made some friends, some enemies, learned how to fight those off, then when I was sixteen I left and headed for San Francisco. I lied to you earlier about college. Never went to one, Mark, sorry. The only education I had was from elementary school and what they taught us at the institution."

"I would never have guessed that," Mark said quietly. "You come across as so intelligent."

"Street smarts, mostly. But I did a lot of reading on my own."

The waiter chose that moment to deliver their desserts, and Mark had a chance to study Evan as he smiled up at the server and chatted for a few seconds. Never in a million years would he have guessed that this beautiful, charismatic man had a background like the one he'd just described. If anything, Mark had supposed Evan came from a well-off family and good schooling. He seemed so poised and confident, so sure of his place in the world. How had he managed to overcome such adversity so early in his life?

The waiter left and Evan turned his attention back to Mark. "Are you disillusioned by my less-than-stellar past?"

"God, no." Mark shook his head vehemently. "If anything, I have even more admiration for you. To have a rotten start like that and become the man you are now is amazing to me. I never dreamed you had it so rough. But what happened in San Francisco?"

"I was homeless for a while, in and out of shelters, fighting off lechers. You get a different perspective on humanity when you're at the bottom of the barrel. *And then!*" Evan threw his arms wide. "If my life were a movie, there would've been a musical crescendo at that moment…" He chuckled. "I got a lucky break. I just happened to pick up a glossy magazine at one of the shelters. Can't remember which magazine it was. There was an advertisement for young models, male and female, wanted by this big agency. Okay, I knew I wasn't a troll…"

Mark let out a snort of laughter. "A major understatement."

Evan laughed too. "I know, but I didn't want to come across as arrogant. Okay, I knew I was attractive from the looks I'd get from men and women, so I thought, why the hell not? Go for it. I had nothing to lose. Of course, my clothes were hardly model standard, but I managed to scrub up, muss my hair like I saw some male models wear it in photographs and presented myself at the agency."

"And the rest is history!" Mark beamed at him.

"It almost didn't happen. When I got to where the auditions were being held and saw the mass of kids applying for a shot as a model, I nearly ran out of there. There were so many boys and girls, and my God, some of them were breathtaking. I figured I had no chance, but I had nothing else to do that day so I waited and eventually was interviewed—and yes, I got accepted, and for the next seven years I was their top model until—well, I told you 'bout the problem I had. And here I am starting over again, and really happy to do so." He reached for Mark's hand. "And also really happy to have met you."

"That is entirely mutual." Mark raised Evan's hand to his lips and kissed it gently. "Thank you for sharing your story with me." They gazed at each other for a long moment, then Mark said, "Why don't we get the desserts boxed and eat them at your place?"

Evan's eyes glittered in the light shed by the candle on their table. "How about if I eat mine off your very sexy body?"

Mark shivered, and his voice was thick with desire as he murmured, "Let's go."

Chapter Six

Mark called Kyle the following morning to give him the good news about his part in the movie, and almost lost his eardrum again when Kyle screeched on the other end.

"Oh, my God, that is fantastic, Mark. I am so happy for you, happy, happy, happy for you!"

Mark laughed. "You should really learn how to express yourself more fully, Kyle."

"But this is so exciting, Mark. Aren't you excited?"

"Yes, I'm excited."

"You don't sound excited enough!"

"Kyle — this is me, excited."

"Okay, what's the movie called? I'm going on Facebook to let all my five thousand, nine hundred and ninety-one friends know all about it."

"Kyle, you are a hoot. It's called *Burning Hearts* and I play an artist suspected of murder."

"Wow! And did you do it?"

"I don't think so, but now that you ask, I'm not sure." Mark chuckled. "The producer just called. We have a read-through this afternoon, so I guess I'll find out."

"A read-through. God, that sounds so exciting."

"And nerve-racking. The other cast members will be there so I'm a bit nervous about meeting them. They'll have done movies before and —"

"And you'll be perfect and they'll love you."

"From your mouth, as the saying goes. I have met the guy playing the detective…Evan Ericson. You heard of him?"

"No. Is he hot?"

"Very hot. Beautiful, actually, and really nice. We…uh,

we had dinner last night."

"Hmm. The way you said that makes me think it was more than just dinner. Tell me, Mark — were you the dessert?"

Mark chuckled. "Subtle, aren't you?"

"I nailed it — you had sex with him! Oh, my God, Mark, quite the change in your routine. A movie part, and a man in your life, at long last. I love it!"

"Hardly, Kyle. I've only known him two days. Well, today makes three. He is terrific, though. So, enough about me, how'd your date with sourpuss go?"

"He's not so sour," Kyle told him. "Kinda sweet actually. He's just really serious about life, and politics and shit like that."

"Please tell me he's not a Republican."

"No, he's not. Gay Republican, that's funny. Anyway, we had a nice time at dinner then he walked me home." Kyle giggled. "Well, of course he had to as we live in the same apartment. We kissed — and then he went to his room and I went to mine."

"And there was a knock on your door around midnight?"

"No, nothing like that. But I have hopes that he'll want to ravish this perky body of mine one of these days, so watch this space."

After they ended their call, Mark took a long shower then picked out a clean pair of blue jeans and opted for a dark-brown shirt. Just in case he sweated from nerves, he figured the color would disguise any evil pit stains. Standing in front of the mirror to comb his hair, he remembered a moment from the night before when Evan had stood behind him, resting his chin on Mark's shoulder and gazing into his eyes through the mirrored reflection after they'd showered together.

It had been another perfect night with Evan. The guy was just such an amazing lover, so warm and tender one minute, dominant the next, without being overly rough. He did like to wrestle, though. Liked being on top, to pin Mark under him, hold him there while he kissed the bejesus out of him, and Mark liked him doing that just fine. He was hard just thinking about it. God, he'd never had so much sex in such a short span of time—real sex, anyway. What had passed between Corey and him could never really be called sex. Yes, he'd given the jerk a blow job a few times, and Corey had fucked him once or twice. Twice in two years, and had done such a shit awful job of it, Mark had thought he'd never want to have anal sex again. He must have been out of his mind. The difference between Corey and Evan could be measured in light years.

And that amazing story he'd told Mark. Who would have guessed that Evan had suffered such an awful childhood? It made his own experiences at home seem almost inconsequential in comparison. At least his parents had given him a decent enough upbringing. Going to church hadn't really been that much of a hardship. He'd had fun watching and joining in with the other kids' antics while listening to the pastor drone on about Hell and damnation. Even the slap on the back of his head from his mother when she'd caught him at it hadn't really upset him. It had been over and forgotten, as quickly as it had happened...most times.

The chime of his cell phone got his attention back to the present and he smiled when he saw Evan's name on the screen. "Hey, how are you?"

"Just the best."

Mark chuckled. "You don't have to tell me. I know you're the best."

Evan joined in the chuckling. "I meant I was feeling the best. After last night, how could I not? And you left before I could fuck you again. No fair, Mark."

"My poor ass needed a rest."

"Oh, sorry. But we're good for tonight, yes?"

Laughter bubbled up inside Mark. "Do you ever think of anything else?"

"Of course I do, just not when I think of you and that delicious butt of yours. I want to bury my face in there and tongue you to death."

"Evan!" Mark groaned. "How is it possible you can make me hard just by talking to me?"

"That's what phone sex is all about."

"Not going to happen. We have the read-through in an hour and I want to look over my lines so I don't sound like an amateur in front of the other cast members. Hey, by the way, I only have part of the script here. D'you know if I'm the murderer?"

Evan's chuckle was evil. "No, it's me – and I lure you into my web with lies and deceit, then I kill you."

"What? You're kidding!"

Evan laughed out loud. "Yes, I am. Richard wants to tell us at the read-through."

"Oh, okay. I'm hoping that we have a happy ending."

"*Are* you now?"

"I-in the movie, I mean." Mark knew he sounded flustered. *Dammit!*

"Well, I'm hoping for that too."

Evan's words hung in the air between them. *He didn't say 'in the movie'.*

"Uh…um, okay, I'll see you at the production office then."

"You most certainly will. *Ciao, bambino.*"

Mark laughed. "Later."

His phone chimed again just as he was getting ready to leave. "Mark Henderson."

"Hey, Mark, it's Brett Lester. From the Ron Lester office?"

"Oh hi, how're you?"

"Good. Dad told me you got the part, and I just wanted to call and say congratulations."

"That is so nice of you. Thanks."

"How's it going?"

"Well, so far so good. Really exciting in fact. I'm just on my way to meet the rest of the cast and do the first read-through of the script with them."

"That sounds so fucking rad. I am really jealous, but wish you all the best." Brett sighed. "If I could just get my old man to let me audition for stuff, I know I would be good."

"I'm sure you'll get your chance one of these days." Mark wasn't sure of anything of the sort, but Brett had been nice, ultimately, and from the sounds of it needed a little boost to his spirits. "If I hear of anything upcoming I'll call to let you know."

"That would be terrific of you, thanks. Good luck today. I'm looking forward to seeing the movie when it's released. Keep in touch."

"Will do. Bye, Brett."

* * * *

To say Mark was nervous when he walked into the Light in the Forest production office was putting it mildly. He was going to have to shake hands with people and his palms were sweaty. *How totally embarrassing*. There was a restroom next door so he ducked in there to wash his hands. Maybe if he held them under the dryer long enough? There was a man standing at a urinal. *Evan*.

"Hey, Mark. You're looking mighty sharp."

"Thanks, you too." Sharp was an understatement when it came to Evan's appearance. He was wearing a white T-shirt that molded to his torso perfectly and a pair of black jeans that emphasized his muscular thighs. Add to that a pair of cowboy boots and he was every inch the stud. And Mark could still feel those inches, and relished every one.

"Bit nervous, though." Mark headed for the first sink and turned on the water. He soaped up and gave his hands a thorough wash. Evan joined him at the next sink and flashed him a smile as he also washed his hands.

"I'm nervous too," Evan said and leaned over to kiss Mark's cheek.

"You?"

"Yes, me. Don't forget I'll be under the microscope from these other guys. The unknown entity. The one who could throw this movie under the bus if he doesn't come up to expectations."

Mark rinsed off. "Don't think there's any danger of that. You've already proved yourself to Richard and Charles." He walked over to the dryer and turned it on, holding his hands under the hot blast of air. "That's all that matters at this stage, I should think."

Evan came up behind him and kissed his neck. "I love that you're so supportive of me." He pulled a paper towel from the dispenser and dried his hands. He waited until Mark was through with the dryer then dragged him into his arms and delivered a knee-melting kiss to Mark's lips. Mark groaned and gave himself up to the sensuousness of Evan's mouth and body pressed to his.

"God, Evan," he muttered when they finally broke apart. "Look what you've done." He pointed at the bulge behind his zipper.

Evan chuckled. "Me too." He rubbed the front of Mark's jeans. "I should get on my knees and worship it, but we're expected in about one minute, so..." He touched his lips to Mark's lightly. "Let's go."

Slightly dazed by Evan's actions, Mark followed him, glad he could go in to face the others with Evan instead of by himself. Seven men of all ages and shapes and one blonde woman turned to stare at them as they entered. Charles, Roger and Richard he recognized, but the rest? Charles came over, all smiles.

"Ah, here they are. Everyone, I'd like to introduce Evan Ericson and Mark Henderson. Evan is portraying our detective, Jeff Hollister, and Mark is the artist, Peter Jennings." He turned and grasped the hand of the blonde. "Marsha Simmons, meet Evan and Mark."

Marsha's smile was a little tight, but Mark figured she might be nervous too. The four men—Mark tried to remember all the names—were Gregory Mathis, an older man who looked familiar, Troy Cunningham, attractive, but with a cocky attitude, Sam Barnes, sharp features, long nose and a mustache and Barry Whitfield, a tall African-

American with a ready smile and a hearty handshake.

As Pamela, the script coordinator, slipped into the room, Charles said, "Okay, if you'll take your seats at the table, we'll get started. Richard is going to give you all a brief synopsis of the story and then we'll start reading."

"Good morning, everyone." Richard stood at the end of the table, script already open. "This movie, *Burning Hearts*, is my dream come true. I wrote the screenplay three years ago and pitched it to so many studios I swear I wore out three pairs of shoes."

Polite titters followed his remark.

"Ultimately, I decided to make the film myself, or at least gather as much financial support as I could, put my own money into it, and with Charles' help and encouragement, here we finally are. We are very lucky to have Charles as our director. Everyone in the business already knows his fine work, and Roger King, our cine-photographer, has received several awards over the years. I have also been very lucky in that a dear friend of mine, Michael Roberts, is writing the musical score. So, with these important positions filled by real pros, I feel we are on the road to success."

Richard paused and looked around the table, smiling at his cast. "You can see from the number of people assembled here that this is a small-budget movie, like most indies. Many of the shots will be tight, sets minimal, stock film of outdoor scenes will be used. I have already got that set up with Roger's help. Today we have a simple cold reading, no need to show your acting chops. You have all been chosen for the roles because Charles and I think you are right for them.

"The story is set in the fifties." Richard cleared his throat then continued, "It involves the murder of a scandal sheet columnist, the ensuing investigation by a detective, a Korean War veteran with his own secrets, and a gay tryst. Marsha plays Samantha Goodall, the columnist who is found murdered after a more-than-salacious article she has written about a closeted star Clark Cooper, played by our own Gregory here, causes quite the uproar in the Hollywood community. Her much younger boyfriend Joe Banks, played by Troy, fingers an up-and-coming artist, Peter Jennings — that's Mark's role — and tells the detective, Jeff Hollister — as I mentioned before, that's Evan's part — that he suspects Peter is the murderer."

During the reading, Mark watched the actors as they read their parts, impressed by the assuredness they projected. Even though they were not required to act out their roles, Gregory and Marsha injected their lines with just enough flair to inform the rest of them that they better step up to the plate when it came time to be in front of the cameras. Mark had a short, heated scene with Gregory as the aging movie star Clark Cooper. Mark was glad he'd had time to read this part of the script so that the intensity of the words didn't throw him.

"Okay, we'll take a little break here," Richard announced and gave Mark a thumbs up.

Mark breathed a sigh of relief.

"You are so good," Evan whispered and put his arm around Mark's shoulders. "Let's get some coffee."

They got up from the table together and Mark noticed that Troy was eyeing Evan with more than just a passing interest. *Oh well, that's bound to happen,* he thought, but at least Evan didn't seem to be paying the guy much attention.

As the reading progressed, Troy and Evan had their scene together, Marsha already having been dispatched, and Mark was amused by the fact that Troy overacted a bit, getting vehement about Peter, the artist, being involved in the murder. When it came to Mark and Evan's scene, after the dialog, Richard, who was giving brief action directions, said, "Jeff grabs Peter and kisses him." Evan leaned toward Mark and kissed him full on the lips.

There was some good-natured chuckling then Troy said, "Quite the wild man, aren't you, Evan."

Mark was tempted to reply with, 'You have no idea how wild', but thought it best to let it go. Evan, still looking at

Mark, rolled his eyes, and ignored the remark.

"Okay, that's good for now," Charles said. "Take a lunch break, everyone. Good work, all of you."

Gregory Mathis came over and clapped Mark on the shoulder. "Richard tells me this is your first film."

"That's right."

"Well, you're doing just fine. I liked the way you countered my accusations, coming in just before I finished. It came across as a spontaneous reaction, which translates really well on the screen. You must have done some stage work."

"Yes, sir."

"Gregory, please." The older man laughed. "Don't make me feel older than I look."

"You look great," Evan said. "Very silver fox."

Troy suddenly appeared alongside them "You guys wanna go get a drink? There's a bar on the corner. They serve food too."

"Sounds like a plan." Evan put a proprietary arm around Mark's waist and headed for the door. "Richard, Charles… you guys comin'?"

"No, we're going to take a look at some of the dialog we think needs tightening up," Charles replied. "You can bring us back a sandwich, if you don't mind."

Once outside, Marsha excused herself, saying she had another appointment and would see them back in an hour.

"She doesn't like me," Evan murmured close to Mark's ear as they walked to the bar on the corner. "Richard felt it only right that the others knew of my porn career and she voiced her disapproval. Far as I know, she's the only one who did."

"But she didn't back out, so she can't mind that much," Mark said.

"She probably needs the money."

Mark observed the others walking ahead of them, chatting amiably among themselves. "I think they already consider us a couple. I hope you don't mind that."

"'Course not. You can bet they'll use that as part of the

publicity. 'Lovers on the set, and in real life'."

"You think? The gay angle is only a small part of the movie, from what I've read of the script."

"Yeah, but once the gay press gets wind of our nude love scene, it'll become the major part." Evan chuckled. "Can't think why, though. Most of them will have seen my bare ass before."

"But it's an ass that bears seeing way more than once or twice. Personally, I don't think I'll ever get tired of looking at it."

Laughing, they followed the others into the bar.

* * * *

As the first week slid into the next they moved to a larger studio where the film would be shot. Mark was feeling more relaxed around the other cast members, and even Marsha seemed to have mellowed—no doubt impressed with Evan's acting ability and professionalism, he thought. On his first day of actual filming, though, he felt his nervousness return, especially as Evan wasn't there to give his confidence a boost. Mark's scene was with Marsha and Troy.

Marsha was word-perfect and knew her marks on set with an instinct he envied. He and Evan had rehearsed their lines together, Mark filling in for the other characters Evan, as Jeff Hollister, was interrogating. His scene with Marsha and Troy went fairly well, although Charles didn't seem too pleased with Troy's performance.

"Oh, dear," Marsha muttered as they watched Charles gesticulating while he talked with Troy in a corner of the studio. "Lover boy is going to have to put out some more if he wants to stay on Charles' good side."

Mark almost choked. "Charles and Troy?"

Marsha gave him a raised eyebrow stare as if to say, 'Surely you jest?' "You didn't know? I suppose you also didn't know that Troy was furious you got the part he wanted. Bigger part, of course, but it was the chance of having a romantic scene with Evan that made him salivate. Now that I've seen Evan I don't blame him. You two doing it, then?"

Mark almost choked again. "Uh…"

"That's what I thought." Marsha chuckled. "Well, I'm sure you boys are having way more fun than the rest of us."

"You're married, aren't you?" Mark asked.

"That's what I mean, honey…" She fell silent as Troy rejoined them, looking not very happy, and Frank yelled for everyone to take their places.

The gist of the scene with Marsha and Troy was that Mark, as the artist, Peter, had been commissioned by Samantha Goodall, Marsha, to paint her portrait. Troy, as her boy-toy, Joe, tried to put the make on Peter, who rebuffed him, but not before Samantha walked in and saw Joe and Peter in what could have been construed as a compromising situation. The row that followed was short but intense, and in the process Troy grabbed Mark's arm so viciously that when he wrenched it away he knocked over the easel and canvas.

"Cut!" Charles advanced on them and Mark rubbed at his arm where Troy had grabbed him.

"That wasn't bad," Charles said, "but don't overplay it, Troy. You all right, Mark?"

"Yeah, sure. Troy just doesn't know his own strength, I guess."

"Okay, we'll do that again. Get ready for another take."

Troy mumbled, "Sorry. I guess I was really trying to get into the part."

"It's called overacting, dear," Marsha said, and Troy scowled at her.

Charles seemed more pleased with the second take, though Mark noticed him frown as he said, "Mark, it's your scene with Gregory next. Clear the set!" Charles walked away like a man with a loaded schedule to get through. Mark watched as the crew set up for the next scene which represented Clark Cooper's study. A desk and chairs were wheeled in and bookshelves arranged strategically behind them. Gregory came to stand by him as they waited for Charles to call them to their marks.

"How are you today?" Gregory asked, touching Mark's arm lightly.

"Good, thanks." Mark liked Gregory. The older man was handsome, but it was his quiet professionalism that Mark admired more. Something he hoped to develop one day, if he managed to keep working long enough in movies or theatre.

"I saw young Troy getting a bit rough with you earlier."

"Oh, he was just a little over-exuberant, that's all."

"I don't care for unscripted moves," Gregory said.

Mark wondered what Gregory would have thought of Evan's unscripted move the day of Mark's audition. Charles called on them at that moment and they walked over to the set to prepare. Once the lights and sound were in place, Charles called, "Action!"

Gregory leaned against a mahogany desk as he delivered his first line.

Clark: I thought you were my friend, Peter.

Peter (*impatiently*): I am your friend.

Clark: Yet you agreed to paint that bitch's portrait. She's out to ruin me, you know, and if that column is printed, your name will appear in it alongside mine. You know what they say about guilt by association, don't you?

Peter (*shrugs*): I don't think anyone is going to be interested in the life of an unknown painter. Unknown, and broke enough to paint Jack the Ripper's portrait, if he were alive, and had the money!

"Cut!" Charles came over. "You guys are fine, but the lighting's not right. Relax while I get that taken care of, then we'll go again."

Pamela and Claire descended on them, Pamela to huddle

with Gregory over some script points while Claire mussed up Mark's hair to her satisfaction.

* * * *

The rest of the morning went by quickly enough and Charles seemed pleased with what they had all done. Mark's stomach rumbled and he glanced at his watch. *Almost lunch time, thank goodness.* He glanced over as the door at the far end of the studio opened, and Evan strolled in. Wearing a pale blue polo and khaki chinos, his blond hair gleaming under the studio lights, he looked amazing, and Mark felt a tightening in his chest as the man walked toward him. Mark knew he was falling for Evan, but then why wouldn't he? It might not be the smartest thing he'd ever done, but the time he spent in Evan's company only helped increase the affection he felt for him.

"Hi there." Evan grinned at him then leaned in to kiss his cheek. "I've come to take you to lunch, unless you have a better offer already."

"No better offer…yet. But lunch is on me. I got a paycheck."

Evan chuckled. "Good. Lemme just go talk with Charles, then we can eat."

Mark watched him move across the soundstage with that model-elegant grace of his, and as always, his gaze fixed on Evan's ass. *It is a thing of beauty…* A low whistle off to his side had him turning to see Troy, a lascivious stare also fixed on Evan's butt.

"You're getting some of that, aren't you?"

"Excuse me?" Mark didn't even try to hide his annoyance. "That's a bit crass, isn't it?"

Troy shrugged. "It's not like no one knows what's going on with you two."

"It isn't really anybody's business, and sure as hell doesn't excuse what you said."

"Oh, get over yourself, Mary. Go learn how to act."

Mark laughed. "That, coming from you, is a joke. You're

the one who was overacting all over the damn place earlier."
Mark cringed inwardly after he'd said the words. He really
didn't want to get into a bitch-fest with Troy. They were
going to be working together for the next few weeks. *Better
apologize...* "Look..."

"Fuck off," Troy snarled and stomped away just as Evan
arrived.

"What's wrong with him?"

"Oh, shit. He was rude and I kinda snapped his head off.
I shouldn't have, I guess."

Evan took his arm and they walked to the exit together.
"Rude about what?"

Mark sighed. "You and me. He said everyone knows
what's going on between us."

"That's not his business."

"That's what I told him, then he got nasty, and... Oh, hell,
let's forget it. I don't want it spoiling our lunch date."

"Nor will it. Troy's a bit of an ass. Just ignore him." Evan
pulled him into the corridor outside the soundstage and
kissed him, hard. "Better?" he asked when they came up
for air.

Mark smiled. "Much."

"Good. Let's go eat."

* * * *

Evan's favorite diner was close by so they decided to take
a leisurely stroll there and enjoy the sunny, though cool,
weather of the day. Evan slipped his hand over Mark's as
they walked. Not something Mark would have dreamed of
doing in Spokane, Washington. *But hey, this is Los Angeles,
California,* he thought. Neither of them paid much attention
to the guy approaching until he suddenly had a camera in
his hand and had taken three rapid shots of them in quick
succession.

"Thanks, guys," he said with an almost manic grin on his
face. "Good follow-up to this." He thrust a newspaper into

Evan's hand then took off before they could protest.

"What the hell?"

Evan glanced at the front page of the paper and frowned. "It's a scandal sheet." The headline was some bullshit about Prince Harry defying his grandmother to date an American billionaire's daughter, the photograph so out of focus and scratchy it could have been anyone. Evan was about to throw it in a nearby trash bin when Mark asked, "What's that in the corner, down there? It looks a bit like you."

"Passionate farewell at LAX, story page nine." Evan growled. "Shit, it's a picture of me and Dareck at the airport." He quickly turned to page nine and there it was, a really clear photograph of Dareck kissing him on the lips. The caption read, *Porn Star Lovers Bid Each Other Adieu*. Evan sighed. "Crap."

Evan read the rest of the article as they walked to the diner. "Porn stars Dean Masters and Dareck Dante are caught on camera as they say a fond farewell. Dareck was leaving for parts unknown. Dean, who now masquerades under the name Evan Ericson—assholes, that's my name!" he interjected bitterly. He glanced at Mark. "Sorry. Anyway, blah, blah, blah… Masters or Ericson looked dejected as he waved his lover *au revoir*. Maybe his new part in a legit movie will cheer him up. Our source tells us he is starring in *Burning Hearts*, an indie movie directed by Charles Bennett. Does Mr. Bennett know he hired a porn actor for the part? Does this mean *Burning Hearts* will be retitled *Crash and Burn Hearts*? We can't wait to find out!"

They had reached the diner, but Evan paused in pushing the door open. "You still hungry?"

Mark shook his head. "Not really."

"I think I need a drink."

"Just one, though," Mark said. "You have scenes this afternoon."

"Yeah…" Evan sighed. "That." They set off toward a bar a few yards from the diner. "I wonder if Richard and Charles will still want me after they read this piece of crap."

"Evan, they know you worked in porn. I imagine they would take into consideration this kind of thing happening. The paparazzi love to stir up shit like this, especially when it involves gays."

They stepped inside the bar, the dimness startling in contrast to the brilliant sunshine outside. "I think I'll have a Scotch." Evan pulled out his billfold. "What about you?"

"Just a glass of wine…white."

He wandered over to an empty booth and slumped down onto the padded leather seat. *Dareck is Evan's lover. He said he was just a friend.* He managed to smile when Evan brought their drinks to the table and sat next to him.

"Mark, I'm sorry about this."

"It's not your fault." He had to say it. "So, Dareck and you are lovers?"

"What?" Evan grimaced then took a long swig of his drink. "God, no. Dareck was one of the first guys I worked with in porn. He was a little lost, naïve. Like I told you, not very bright, and I kinda looked after him, I guess is what you'd call it. But outside of him and me doing it on film, nothing else happened between us."

Mark felt a rush of relief at Evan's words.

"Mark…" Evan stared at him, his expression serious. "I know in my life I've done what some people would definitely frown on—but I don't cheat. If Dareck had been my lover, I'd never have put the make on you, gorgeous as you are. Okay?"

Mark nodded, feeling suitably foolish and chastised. "I'm sorry. It…it was just reading that in the article."

"Right, and most likely ninety percent of those who read it will believe it too. That's what sells their crappy tabloids."

"And that guy who took our picture with us holding hands…"

"Yeah, most likely that'll be in the next edition. Dean Masters slash Evan Ericson has found a new beau now that his lover is in parts unknown! When the cat's away, the rats will play! Bastards."

Mark forced a chuckle. "I think it's the mice will play."

"Is it? I think I'd rather be a rat than a mouse—bigger, feistier." He threw back the rest of his drink. "We better head back and give them the news before someone else does. They'll want to have a statement prepared to ward off the gossips." He leaned over and kissed Mark's cheek. "Come on, gorgeous, let's go."

Chapter Seven

When they got back to the studio it seemed that everyone was already aware of the article. One of the crew had picked up a copy of the tabloid while at lunch. Charles and Richard were fairly upbeat about it.

"Look at it this way," Richard said, shrugging. "Oscar Wilde was of the opinion that the only thing worse than being talked about was *not* being talked about."

"So you're not mad?" Evan asked

"Not at you." Charles threw the copy of the tabloid on the table in front of him. "And Richard's right. This will cause a stir in the gossip industry and that's all free publicity."

"What I can't understand" — Marsha put on a pair of glasses to peer at the photograph of Evan and Dareck — "is why in this day and age, and especially here in California, this should be newsworthy. Everyone knows, or should know by now, that gays exist. When I was younger it was known as the love that dare not speak its name — now it's the love that won't shut up!"

Everyone laughed. "I think this might be news in some areas of the country," Charles said, "but pretty much a non-event around here."

"Some guy took a picture of us outside," Mark told him. "We were uh...holding hands."

Marsha gasped in mock horror. "Oh no, not that."

"That's great," Pamela said. "We can use that... 'Lovers on set and off!'"

"Yeah, but..."

Mark and Evan turned at the sound of Troy's snarky tone.

"You're all taking this very lightly," Troy continued, "but

you know how it is in Hollywood. They all go out of their way to deny anything gay, even when they're playing gay characters. It's macho or *nada*."

"Well, that won't be the case here," Charles said brusquely. "No one will deny anything. This movie involves gay characters played by gay actors and that's how it will be portrayed, if and when the rest of the press shows interest in this article. Richard and I will prepare a statement for that purpose. Now, I think we've wasted enough time on this. We have a movie to make!"

Mark stayed on to watch Evan's next two scenes. One where, as the detective, he questioned Gregory about his involvement with Samantha Goodall, the murder victim, and the second with Sam Barnes and Barry Whitfield, who played his fellow cops. For budget reasons the sets were pretty basic, and Mark wondered if the movie would suffer from looking cheap, but when he saw the rushes later, he was truly impressed. Under Charles' skillful direction, mood-driven lighting and Roger's sharp camera work the scenes had been given a tight film noir feel that worked especially well in close-ups. Evan, of course, looked terrific, his nuanced facial expressions saying even more at times than the dialog.

Mark found that he was holding his breath, caught up in Evan's intensity. He jumped when Charles called out his name. "Mark, we're gonna have time for your scene with Evan. Go see Claire and get ready, please." Evan gave him a thumbs up as he rushed off to Wardrobe.

"Sorry," he said to Claire, "wasn't expecting to be used again today."

Claire glanced at her watch. "We're ahead of schedule. Pamela told me Charles is so pleased with the fact he can call a wrap after two or three takes of Evan's scenes. He's really good, isn't he?"

Mark nodded as he slipped on the paint-spattered shirt he needed for this scene. "He's a scene-stealer, all right. He's just so quietly powerful, if you know what I mean. This is the first time we're on camera together and I'm nervous as a cat." He sat patiently while Claire dusted his face with powder and rearranged his hair.

"You'll be fine," she said. "You two look great together, by the way. I have a feeling this movie will pull in a bunch of awards."

"That'd be great." *Great for all of us, but especially for Evan… He so wants to succeed in this business.* "Thanks, Claire."

"Go kill 'em out there."

The set had been transformed from the police precinct to Peter's studio. His easel and canvas stood in front of a large screen backlit to represent a window. At Charles' signal Mark walked onto the set and took his position with his back to the window. Some art supplies were scattered around and a cane chair stood just inside the 'doorway'. As rehearsed previously, there would be a close-up of Mark trying to show disinterest in Evan's presence. The camera would then pan over to where Evan sat astride the cane chair, watching Mark.

"And, action!"

Jeff: All I'm trying to do is ascertain your whereabouts the night Samantha Goodall was murdered.

Evan's voice was low, deliberate and very sexy.

Feigning impatience, Mark put down the prop paint palette and brush he was holding then turned to face Evan. *God, he is so fucking hot…* His voice trembled slightly.

Peter: And as I told the other detective, I was here, working on Samantha's portrait. Not that it will be needed now.
Jeff: Did you finish it?
Peter: No.

As they rehearsed, they stared at each other for a long moment, each man realizing their now mutual attraction.

Mark knew Roger and his assistant would be taking close-ups of first him, then Evan. He had no trouble whatsoever emoting while gazing at Evan.

Charles yelled, "Cut! Let's go back to 'did you finish it'. Ready, Roger?"

"Yep."

Jeff: Did you finish it?
Peter: No.
Jeff: Why not?
Peter: The woman's dead. What's the point? No one will pay my commission, certainly not her boy-toy.
Jeff: You think he did it?
Peter: How the hell would I know?

A pause, as directed.

Peter: I don't think he'd have the guts for it. For murder, or even for blackmail.
Jeff: And you would?
Peter: You're an ass, Detective. What is it about me that makes you think I had anything to do with blackmailing or murdering Samantha Goodall? I told your other goon when we talked that I barely knew the woman. She was a client, is all. Now you're acting as if I'm the only suspect. Let's get this straight once and for all, I did not blackmail her, nor did I kill her!

Evan got up off the chair and gave Mark a predatory smile.

Jeff: Has anyone told you you're kind of hot when you get all defensive?
Peter: Detective…

As in the script's directions, Mark raised an eyebrow in derision.

Peter: You are not scoring any brownie points with me using that type of approach. Apart from it being inappropriate, it's cheesy at best.

Evan moved closer to Mark.

Jeff: Cheesy, huh?

He chuckled and reached out to undo the buttons on Mark's shirt.

Jeff: I guess I'll have to improve my pick-up lines. How about this?

Charles had wanted to keep the part where Evan ripped Mark's shirt open in rehearsal. Evan tore Mark's shirt open, pulled him into his arms and kissed him, long and hard.

After a few beats, as directed, Mark pushed him back.

Peter: What the hell are you doing?
Jeff: It's called kissing, Peter Painter, and you love it.

"Cut!" Charles strode over to the set. "That was great. We just need some extra shots, so we'll go back to where Mark calls you an ass. Okay?"

The extra shots took a long time and Mark was alternately aroused by Evan's kisses, the fact he could feel the man's erection pressing against his own, and exhilarated by the thrill that this was all really happening. He was acting, and was going to appear in an actual movie. By the end of the shoot, he was worn out. The kissing scene had been repeated several times, not that either one of them had complained. Charles had wanted an overhead shot of the two of them in the clinch and that had taken time to set up. Finally, though, Charles was satisfied and called it a wrap.

"Good work, boys. That's it for today. At some point tomorrow, not sure when yet, probably morning, we'll get to your love scene. I'd like that to be as unrehearsed as possible…" He winked at them. "But feel free, you know, on your own time."

Mark blushed, Evan laughed and Troy scowled.

* * * *

By mutual consent, they decided to go their separate ways after they left the studio. On the way back to his apartment, Mark realized he was starving. Why hadn't he suggested they get a bite to eat together before going home? Come to think of it, why hadn't Evan suggested it? *Maybe he's pissed because I asked if he and Dareck were lovers.* Evan certainly hadn't acted pissed when they'd been in that scene together. Evan had kissed him like there might be no tomorrow. Then again, he had been acting. He was a damn good actor…

"Oh, for Chrissakes," he yelled at himself out loud. "Evan's not the kind of guy to act pissy over something like that. I apologized and he seemed to be okay with it." *But what if he wasn't? He said, 'I don't cheat', and he'd sounded hurt. Oh, fuck.* He pulled into the drive-thru lane of an Arby's and ordered a turkey and cheese sandwich on wheat with curly fries. While he waited he punched in Evan's number on his cell.

"Are you home?" he asked when Evan answered.

"Yeah. What's up?"

"Are we okay? I got to thinking maybe I'd made you mad earlier when I asked if you and Dareck were lovers. I'm sorry if I did."

Evan chuckled. "I'm not mad, but I thank you for caring enough to call and ask. We're good, Mark. No worries."

It was hearing Evan say those words that made Mark realize just how much he did care for the man. In the weeks that they'd worked so closely together, so intimately at times, Mark had come to not only admire Evan for his talent, but to also have deep feelings for him. It would have torn him up if their friendship had been compromised because of what he'd said.

"Are *you* okay?" Evan asked.

"Yeah, better now I've talked to you."

"Have you eaten?"

"I'm at the Arby's pick-up window. You want I should get you something? I could bring it over." *Please don't think I'm being pushy…*

"Sounds ideal. I'll have whatever you're having."

Mark breathed out a sigh of relief. "I'll see you in a few." Grinning like a kid, he signaled the attendant and told her he wanted to make that a double order.

* * * *

When Evan opened the door to his apartment Mark could tell he'd just showered. His light-blond hair was darker from being only towel dried. He was wearing a sleeveless T-shirt and a pair of skimpy shorts and, Mark thought, he looked good enough to eat. He grabbed the Arby's bags from Mark, set them on the entry hall table then pushed a surprised Mark up against the wall and kissed him, his tongue entering Mark's open mouth and making him see stars.

"Wow," he gasped when Evan broke the kiss. "Don't think I'll ever get enough o' that."

"Good." Evan grinned. "'Cause there's a lot more where *that* came from." He took Mark's hand, picked up the bags and led him into the kitchen. "I am fucking starving, and didn't even think of it until I got back. Thank you. You're a lifesaver. Oooh…" His grin got bigger when he pulled out the curly fries. "My favorite!"

Mark groaned silently. *I am so in love with you…*

"Like a beer?"

Mark had to clear his throat before saying, "Please."

"Go sit." Evan nodded at the bar stools on the other side of the counter then went to get the beer from the fridge.

Moments later they were chowing down on delicious sandwiches and fries, both of them making sounds of appreciation as though they were dining at the Ritz.

"So…" Evan wiped his mouth with a napkin. "Big day for us tomorrow. You nervous?"

"It'll be different,"' Mark said. "It's not like we haven't done it before, just not with other people in the room."

"Yeah. The first porn I did, it was weird. I'm naked, the guy I'm doing it with — Dareck, by the way — is naked. We have guys all around us, bright lights…too bright. You wouldn't believe the camera angles they go for." He chuckled. "At least we won't have to put up with that. Charles isn't going to want close-ups of our dicks. Don't worry, it'll be fine."

"I just hope I remember my dialog when you're lying on top of me. No way am I not going to get an erection. You do that to me when I look at you."

"That's sweet." He leaned across and kissed Mark. "Mmm, greasy lips." He took his time licking Mark's lower lip.

"Will it be a closed set, d'you think?" Mark asked when he got his breath back.

"Well, as much as they can do. They still need cameras, lights and sound guys. Charles will probably tell the other actors not to show until their scheduled time."

"Good. I don't want fuckin' Troy there, that's for sure."

"Don't let him get to you, Mark." Evan took his hand and rubbed it gently. "He's Charles' pet right now, and trying to be more than that. Okay…" He slipped off the bar stool and began clearing up their mess.

"Let me do that," Mark said.

"No. Why don't you go take a shower? It'll help soothe you and get you over the stress of the day. Then…" He winked mischievously at Mark. "Then we could rehearse for our big scene tomorrow. What d'ya say?"

Mark laughed. "Only a damn fool would turn down that offer."

Evan patted Mark's ass. "Good boy. See you in the

bedroom in five minutes."

Evan leaned on the bedroom doorjamb and took in the sight of Mark standing in the middle of the room waiting for him. *I don't think the guy knows just how beautiful he is. That lean physique, so nicely defined and toned, that gorgeous hair of his, dark and thick and made for running my fingers through – and those eyes. I get hard just remembering how they are when he looks at me. So intense...* Evan sighed. *I'm falling for him, aren't I? In lust or in love, it doesn't really matter. This is unknown territory for me. It could mean trouble, but he might just be worth it...*

Mark shifted nervously. "Are you coming in, or are you going to stand there looking at me funny like that?"

Evan pushed himself off the jamb. "Be right back." He all but ran into the living room and cued up the stereo console. The liquid sounds of classical guitar filled the room. He hurried back to the bedroom. Mark was sitting on the edge of the bed but stood when Evan entered and walked slowly toward him.

"Just getting you in the mood for our big scene." He put his hands on Mark's hips and tugged him close, letting him feel his already pulsing erection.

"I'm always in the mood, you know that." Mark brushed his lips over Evan's then tilted his head to one side, listening. "What's that?"

"Part of Rodrigo's Guitar Concerto. The perfect music to make love by."

"It's beautiful."

"Like you." Evan kissed him, slow and tender.

Mark trembled in Evan's arms. "You're still wearing too much." He used a line from the film script.

Evan's mouth quirked and he answered in character. "Then why don't you take care of that?"

Mark hooked his thumbs into the waistband of Evan's shorts and yanked them down, sinking to his knees as he slid the shorts over Evan's thighs. Evan's already hard cock slapped Mark lightly on his lips and he parted them, snaking his tongue out to capture the first drops of pre-cum oozing from the slit. Evan shuddered from the sensation of Mark's moist warmth enclosing the head of his cock, and the swift, sensuous glide of his lips down the length, all the way to the root. He cupped Mark's face between his palms and made him look up to see the pleasure he was giving.

The look they shared seemed to sear itself into Evan's soul. He shuddered again, not from the eroticism of Mark's lips but from the realization that what he wanted from Mark was so much more than a blow job, much more than just sex. That sudden awareness made him pull back from Mark's attentions and drop to his knees to wrap Mark in his arms and take his mouth with a kiss that held all his emotions, all of what he wanted Mark to know. That what they were sharing meant more to him than anything he had ever done before in his life, or might ever do in the future.

Mark gasped into Evan's mouth, perhaps surprised by the abrupt change in action, but his arms tightened around Evan and he pressed forward into the kiss, deepening it, his tongue sweeping over Evan's, searching out every corner of his mouth. Evan experienced something new to him while in another man's arms — a rush of joy and delight, yet tinged with apprehension. Words he had never spoken in his life trembled on his lips as they formed in his mind…and even now he hesitated to say them. Was he really ready for this next step? Was Mark ready for it? Would Mark flinch from those words? In the fledging stages of their relationship and new careers, was he ready for a committed involvement?

Mark must have sensed the turmoil in Evan's mind because he leaned back a little and asked, "What's wrong?"

"Nothing's wrong…" He framed Mark's face with his hands and gently ran a thumb over Mark's lush bottom lip. "Except, I think I'm falling in love with you."

Mark blinked. "You are?"

"Yeah. How do you feel about that?"

"I feel…" Mark blushed. "Wait, is this a part of the script

I don't know about?"

Evan smiled. "No, it's not part of the script. It's straight from my heart."

"Oh…" Mark leaned his forehead on Evan's shoulder. "Oh, my God. I love you too, Evan. I have for weeks now, I just didn't want to say it because we're working together and you might not have liked it and—Christ, I'm jibber-jabbering…"

Evan chuckled. "Instead of kissing me."

"I can do that!" Mark pushed Evan onto his back on the floor and lay over him, kissing him like a wild man.

Evan rolled him over onto his side. "Slow down. I'm not going anywhere, sweetheart." He stroked Mark's chest and teased his nipples, one at a time, all the while gazing into Mark's eyes. "You are so beautiful, you know that? Are you going to blush again?"

"Yes, if you say stuff like that."

"I'm going to say it a lot, so get used to it. Along with 'I love you'."

Mark gazed at Evan's face, at the smooth planes of his forehead and cheeks, the blond feathered eyebrows, one partially hidden by a lock of hair that had fallen when Mark had tumbled him onto the floor, those eyes that gazed back at him so earnestly, lovingly, and that mouth that was a sin in itself, so full and lush, made to be kissed over and over. He could look at him forever and never tire of it. So, this is what it felt like to be in love—really in love, not some adolescent craving for a guy who used and abused him. Evan was the antithesis of all things Corey, someone who sure as hell didn't belong in Mark's memory anymore—or in his mind at this precise moment.

Evan stood and offered Mark his hand then pulled him to his feet. "We still have to rehearse," he whispered, his lips on Mark's ear. Mark shivered from the erotic touch and wound his arms around Evan's waist.

"You go first."

"Okay." Evan smiled. "Mind you, we will still have our clothes on at the start of the scene."

"Right, so skip that part. Get to where you push me onto the bed."

"Okay." Evan not so much pushed as lowered Mark onto the bed then lay over him.

"I like that better."

"Yeah, we'll do that tomorrow."

Evan kissed him, slowly trailing his lips across Mark's, easing between them with the tip of his tongue, probing gently, taking his time to thoroughly excite Mark. He slid one hand down the length of Mark's torso until he found that part of him that throbbed and pulsed in his grip. Evan scooted down to take the rigid shaft in his mouth, making love to it with his lips and tongue, sucking, gently at first, then suddenly harder and faster. Mark bucked and he grabbed first at the sheets under him, then at Evan's shoulders, clinging to him as if he were a lifeline. Mark squirmed, his hips arching upward while Evan slid his lips up and down the length of Mark's aching erection with increasing speed. He knew he couldn't last, not when every nerve ending in his body screamed for relief.

"Evan!" The yell that was torn from his throat was followed by his hot cum spilling into Evan's mouth. His body was racked with shuddering jolts as he came and Evan continued to suck until every last drop was wrung from his balls. Evan released him then flung himself over Mark, taking his mouth with a kiss that seemed to sear its way into Mark's soul. Their tongues wrestled together and Mark tasted himself as well as the sweetness of Evan's breath and saliva. Could there ever be anything more intoxicating? Mark wondered as he gave himself up completely to the amazing sensations that poured over and through his entire body.

"God, I love you, Evan." His voice was hoarse, his chest heaving against the solid muscle that pinned him to the mattress. The music Evan had selected now swelled to a stunning climax. How appropriate, he thought, gazing into Evan's lust-filled eyes.

"Fuck me," he whispered.

Evan reached for the lube and smeared the cool gel over and into Mark's entrance. A gentle probing followed then became more forceful when Evan pushed his slick fingers farther inside Mark. He gazed into Mark's eyes, mere millimeters from his own, and sucked in an awed breath at the intensity and desire he saw there. When he pressed his lips to Mark's he knew that Mark had given himself up in total surrender. Mark raised his legs and wrapped them around Evan's torso, allowing him complete access, and his sigh was one of ecstasy as Evan sank his sheathed cock slowly, inch by hard-as-steel inch, into him.

"Yesss…" Mark breathed into Evan's mouth.

Their tongues tangled and they found their rhythm, long thrusting motions back and forth, Mark meeting Evan's body in an erotic bond of fevered skin and rippling muscles. Evan loved this position. He could see his lover's beautiful face flushed with desire, his hooded gaze reflecting the love Evan felt for him.

Evan reached for Mark's cock, already hard again, pulsing in his hand and leaking pre-cum over his fingers. Mark wrapped his arms around Evan's neck and pulled him down for a lingering, searing kiss that threatened to take Evan over the edge. Mark shuddered under him using his hands to claw and stroke his way up and down the length of Evan's spine. Evan gasped into Mark's mouth.

Close, so close.

"Come with me," he mumbled against Mark's lips.

Mark arched his body and cried out while forcing himself through the friction of Evan's fist. Hot cum spilled over Evan's hand and he shouted something unintelligible, spiraling out of control into a welcoming oblivion, every part of him racked with wrenching spasms as he emptied himself into Mark's hot depths. Completely sated, they clung to each other, fused at core and mouth, their kiss one of total bliss and lazy, spent passion.

Chapter Eight

It felt odd to Mark to be waking up in his own bed the next morning. Why the hell had he been so insistent about leaving and coming back to this apartment? He'd spent so much time over at Evan's in the past few weeks that the man he loved had even suggested he bring some changes of clothes so that he didn't have to keep coming back here. He groaned, thinking of what he and Evan could be doing right now. Sounds from the kitchen told him either Perry or Andrew was up and about, which he knew meant inquisition time. He'd managed to avoid it so far, as his roommates' schedules kept them at work during most days. For a few moments he considered just hiding in his room till the coast was clear, but no, he couldn't do that. He had to get ready for today's shoot. A very important shoot, for him and Evan, anyway.

After using the bathroom, he threw on the one and only dressing robe he owned then sauntered into the kitchen, where Andrew was making coffee and toasted bagels, from the delicious smell of things.

"Good morning."

Andrew turned and gave him a blank look. "Who are you, and why are you wearing Mark's robe?"

Mark grinned at him. "Are you saying you've missed me that much?"

Andrew sniffed. "Not at all. I just hope that your absence means you're getting laid day and night, otherwise I might imagine you've taken up cat burglary or something just as exciting."

"No, haven't taken up cat burglary." He got a mug from

a cabinet and poured himself some coffee.

"Aha, so you're getting laid day and night?"

"Not day so much…"

Andrew moaned and struck his forehead with the palm of his hand. "Oh, the world is such an unfair place."

"What the hell are you prattling on about now?" Perry stood watching them and shaking his head at Andrew's antics. He glared at Mark. "Welcome back, stranger."

"I had no idea I'd be so missed," Mark said, laughing.

"Long as you pay your rent you can come and go as you please, for all I care," Perry told him, brushing past to get at the coffee. "How's the movie coming along?"

"Really well, thanks. I have a scene to shoot this morning at ten."

"I read that article about Evan and his *lover*," Andrew said pointedly.

"Dareck's not his lover, just someone who was in trouble, and Evan was helping him go home. And we were photographed walking hand in hand by a guy from the same tabloid, so that'll be something else you can read about."

"The producers aren't worried by this kind of publicity?" Perry asked.

"Wait," Andrew yelped, interrupting. "I want to hear more about this hand-in-hand business. Are you dating Evan Ericson?"

Mark nodded. "Yes, we are…uh, in a relationship."

"How exciting!" Andrew hugged him. "I am so happy for you."

Perry rolled his eyes. "Always the hopeless romantic, aren't you? Except in your case it's even worse. You are a *hopeful* romantic."

"And you are a cruel bitch," Andrew hissed.

"Guys…" Mark held up a hand in warning. "It's way too early in the morning for catfights. Thank you, Andrew, I am happy for me too."

"Okay…" Perry leaned against the counter and stared

at them both. "As always, I'll be the one to play devil's advocate..."

"Oh, here we go," Andrew muttered.

"Be quiet. I am happy for you too, Mark, but I must ask, is this wise? You are working together in a very competitive business. After this film, what then? What if he goes on to star in another, and another, and you don't? Or his past career becomes too much for other producers and they don't want to use him, but you go on getting offers?"

"I don't think that'll be a problem for us, Perry..."

"Oh no? Think of all the movie actors' marriages that have gone down the bloody drain for just that reason."

"Well, I think you're getting way ahead of things," Mark said, knowing he sounded a tad defensive.

"I agree." Andrew put an arm around Mark's shoulders. "God's sake, Per, try and be supportive for once of someone making life changes. Mark doesn't want to be a stick-in-the-mud like you. I wish you all the luck in the world, Mark, and I'll be glad to say one day – I knew Mark Henderson when!"

"Oh, dear God." Perry shrugged. "Of course I wish you all the best too. Perhaps I'm just a little more cynical than Happy Drawers here. I'm off to shower. Have a good day, both of you – and Andrew, don't call me Per!"

"He's more cynical because he's been around longer than any of us," Andrew said when Perry was out of range.

"Did something happen to him?" Mark asked. "I mean, something bad that he hasn't gotten over?"

Andrew sighed. "Yeah, I guess. Just don't tell him I told you. He'll kill me."

"Well, if it's that bad, maybe I shouldn't know."

"He wouldn't actually *kill* me." Andrew poured himself another mug of coffee. "Like some?"

Mark nodded and held out his cup. "Please."

"About five years ago, Perry got an offer to appear in a new TV series, something like *NCIS*, and he was to be the lead. Everything was set up, salary agreed on – a big salary—then the producers found out that Perry's gay and they fired him. Bam, just like that. Said no one would believe he could play a womanizer when the news got out he batted for the other team. He was devastated, poor guy, and whether it was because of that incident, or not, he just couldn't seem to land another job. He did a couple of commercials, a tour of *Cinderella*, but since then, nothing. And the bitch of it is, he's really good. I saw him in a play when we first met, and I was really impressed. He had the audience right there in his hands. So I guess that's why he sounded so cynical about your news. His motto is, 'been there, done that, lost it all'."

"Fuck…" Mark felt bad for Perry, and he could so understand why the guy would be disillusioned. Maybe if *Burning Hearts* was a success and Richard wanted to do another movie, maybe he could recommend Perry, and Andrew too, for roles. *That was a lot of 'maybes', but you never know…* "Well, thanks for telling me. I won't mention it ever, unless he brings it up at some point."

"He won't. The only reason I know about is because he got drunk and I was there to pick up the pieces."

"You love him, don't you?"

Andrew nodded. "Yeah, but there's no future in it. He's too broken to ever give himself to anyone—especially me. He regards me as something of a necessary nuisance."

"Oh, I'm sure that's not true."

"And I'm sure it is. He puts up with me because we're both in the same boat at the moment. Two out-of-work gay actors with no foreseeable change in sight, working as waiters, sharing an apartment—stereotypical much?" Andrew sighed. "Anyway, enough of the drama. You have a shoot to get ready for. I hear Per coming out of the bathroom, so it's all yours."

* * * *

As he made his way through traffic to the studio, Mark

couldn't quite shake the feeling of depression that Andrew's story had invoked in him. Was he being naïve in thinking this was really the beginning of a great career for him and Evan? And even more naïve to hope that their love affair would last with all the pressures the business might throw at them? Suddenly, the joy he'd experienced in Evan's arms, their declarations of love for each other, seemed tenuous, fragile. And what if Perry was right about the short careers of gay actors? He'd had a taste of it firsthand, after all.

Oh boy, you better snap out of this before Evan sees you and asks what the hell is wrong. He'll be expecting you to at least look as if something great happened last night.

And it had, and it had been great, better than great. All he had to do was be his usual optimistic self and everything would be all right. *Yeah, everything.*

* * * *

Evan was already on the soundstage talking with Charles and Richard when Mark pushed open the heavy door and entered the studio. After good mornings were exchanged Charles told them to go see Claire and get ready for their scene.

Evan took Mark's hand as they walked to Wardrobe. "How d'you feel today?"

"Good." He squeezed Evan's hand. "If I'm a little off it's because Andrew told me a sad story this morning."

"About what?"

"About Perry, but you can't ever repeat it."

"I don't know the guy, so why would I repeat it?"

"Well, there's a chance you might meet him one of these days, and…"

"Don't worry, the secret's safe with me."

"I'll tell you later," Mark said as Claire beamed at them both.

"'Morning, sunshines."

"Hi, Claire, how's it goin'?" Evan asked.

"Better now I get my Evan and Mark fix. You two are so fantastic together. I just wish I could watch this scene you're doing, but Charles told Pamela and me to hide back here. I didn't think you'd be shy."

Evan chuckled. "I'm not, but my buddy here…"

"I am," Mark said, feeling his face grow hot.

"See, there he goes." Evan leered at him. "And believe me, Claire, he has nothing to be shy about."

Claire laughed. "Oh, I think you just made him blush harder. Okay, boys, let's get you ready."

* * * *

Charles and Richard were waiting for them on set. Apart from Roger and Tim, his assistant, there were only the sound and lighting techs around. All the other actors and crew were scheduled for later in the day.

"Okay, guys, we've already got the close-ups of you, Evan, knocking on the door to the studio and the close-up of Mark registering his surprise, so we're going from when you're both in Peter's studio together. Let's just run that through, okay? From Peter's first line…"

Peter: I didn't think you'd come.

Jeff: Wild horses wouldn't keep me away.

Peter: So, I'm no longer a suspect?

Jeff: I didn't come here to talk about the case. But as you've brought it up…no, you're no longer a suspect.

Peter: Then why did you come?

Jeff: Why d'you think?

"Okay," Charles said, "that's when you grab him by the front of his shirt, haul him in for a kiss…then slow fade to the bedroom scene. So, keep the kiss going until I yell 'cut'. Let's go for a take. Roger, you ready?"

"Yep."

Evan grinned at Mark. "Keep the kiss going? What is he, some kind of slave driver?"

Mark chuckled but swallowed nervously as Charles called lighting cues, then camera, then, "Action!"

Mark gave Evan his first line and they played out the scene as rehearsed. Mark was mesmerized by the glint of lust in Evan's eyes. *God, he is so fucking amazing...* He almost missed his last line but stumbled into it, expecting to hear Charles yell, "Cut!" But no... Then Evan hauled him by the front of his shirt into the kiss. Mark squirmed against Evan's body as Evan's lips crashed into his and their tongues tangled and wrestled in each other's mouths. Mark melted in Evan's arms. *Holy God...* It was as if every kiss Evan and he had ever shared was wrapped up in this one blistering-hot, flesh-on-flesh experience.

If Charles doesn't yell "Cut!" soon, I'm going to come in my pants.

"Cut!"

Mark stepped back from Evan's arms. He was trembling from head to foot, and from the expression on Evan's face he was pretty shaken up too.

"Hang on, boys, don't move," Charles told them.

"I don't think I can survive another kiss like that," Mark whispered.

"Yes, you can," Evan whispered back. "And if they don't like the take, we're gonna have to do it again."

"Okay," Mark said, and they laughed together.

"Come see this, guys."

They hurried over to check out the camera monitor. Roger played the take back for them and Mark marveled at how the camera had caught the intensity from both of them.

"Pause, Roger," Charles said. "Mark, you hesitated on your last line, but I like it."

"It comes across as real," Richard added. "Like you were slightly unsure of what Evan's answer would be."

They watched the rest of the film, and Bart, one of the sound guys, whistled as he studied the kiss.

"I really don't think we can get better that that," Charles said. "That's gonna burn up the screen."

Mark looked at Evan, who was smiling at him. Damn, if he wasn't falling in love all over again.

"All right, take a break while we get the bedroom set up." Charles led them off to one side with Richard. "I'm just going to let you both be spontaneous. You obviously know what you're doing, so just do it. Let us worry about camera angles and lighting, just be yourselves. The scene starts with both of you nude, so go get a couple of robes from Claire so you can cover up till we need you."

"I could've redone that kiss if he'd asked," Evan said as they walked to get the robes from Claire in Wardrobe.

Mark chuckled. "If you kiss me like that when we're naked I might just have an accident. You think you've seen me blush—but I think my face might explode with embarrassment. Don't laugh, I'm not kidding."

"How'd it go?" Claire asked when they entered her domain.

"Good, one take only," Evan told her. "Mark was hoping for another one, of course."

Claire laughed when Mark huffed, "You're just a big tease. And now I have to get naked with you. Pity me, please, Claire."

"No pity, Mark. I'd get naked with both of you, except I'd be the only one enjoying it!" She handed them their robes and they went into a dressing room to strip. Pamela was there when they came out.

"Guess you guys don't need me today," she said. "Charles wants you to use the set dialog as a guideline only. There's no furtherance of the plot in the lines and he seems to think whatever comes out of your mouths will be great."

Evan and Mark looked at each other then burst out laughing. Claire joined in. "Pamela, you say the filthiest things sometimes."

"What? No, I don't. Oh, you guys, I didn't mean *that*."

Claire's cell chimed and she looked at the screen. "Charles is ready for you."

"The big moment is here," Pamela said and they all

laughed again.

They walked on set, this time Peter's loft bedroom. After discarding the robes, they stood face to face by the bed, waiting for Charles to get the lighting to his exact specifications.

"Roll camera — and, action!"

Evan slipped his arms around Mark and kissed him, gently this time, using only the tip of his tongue on Mark's lower lip. Mark let out a shuddering sigh and Evan lowered him onto the bed then lay over him. *Good*, Mark thought, *they'll capture that amazing ass...* Evan rolled onto his back so that Mark was lying on top of him. *Oh, now it's my ass...*

Evan said, "I knew getting this close to you would be something we'd both enjoy."

Oh, yeah...lines.

"Pretty sure of yourself, aren't you?"

Evan kissed him. "Totally sure."

He rolled Mark onto his back again then began tracing his chest with slow, deliberate kisses. Mark bucked in response. He put his hands on either side of Evan's face and eased him back up for another long, languorous kiss. When Evan pulled back a little, Mark let him take the lead. He let him trail kisses over his torso all the way down to his crotch. His cheek grazed the head of Mark's cock and Mark held his breath, willing himself not to lose control. He'd thought he'd have had trouble becoming aroused with other people and cameras all around them. He should have known better. With Evan kissing him, torturing him really with his lips and tongue, how could he not be aroused?

He whimpered then breathed out a sigh of relief when Charles yelled, "Cut!"

"Oh, my God," he muttered, "just in time."

Evan grinned and tugged Mark's cock.

"Stop it," he hissed.

"You are so beautiful," he whispered in Mark's ear, "and I am so in love with you."

Mark couldn't help but smile at his lover. "I love you

too—now please go get my robe before Charles comes over here."

"You guys, that was amazing." Charles beamed at them.

Mark hadn't had time to put the robe on, so he sat demurely on the edge of the bed with the robe covering his privates.

"We'll have to edit it a little, add some more kissing, but the body shots are incredible. Come see for yourself. For a first take, it is beautiful."

A first take...more kissing? Oh boy. Who knew work could be so fantastic?

They watched the take, and Mark was enthralled by the way the lighting and cinematography made their bodies look like works of art...especially Evan's. His skin was like silk, his hair spun gold, his profile...magnificent. He jumped slightly when Evan caressed his nape. "You are fabulous," he whispered, but in Mark's mind the scene belonged to Evan.

"Add some mood music to that," Richard said, "and we have a winner."

"All we have to do is get some more shots of you on the bed." Charles led them back to the set. "Maybe sitting on the side, gazing into each other's eyes, another kiss, a caress of face or hair—well, you both know what to do."

* * * *

"I don't know about you," Evan said, glancing at his watch, "but I could use some lunch and a cold beer. That took longer than I thought it would." They were in the men's restroom, washing up.

Mark chuckled. "It took a lot more out of me than I thought it would. Man, you really had me going there on that third take. Phew. I know my face was red half the time."

"You looked adorable..." His cell phone chimed and he pulled it out of his pocket, frowning at the unfamiliar number on the screen. "Evan Ericson."

"Or is it Dean Masters?" The voice, too, was unfamiliar, but there was a nasty inference behind the question.

"No, this is Evan Ericson. Who is this?"

"This is a friend of Dareck Dante's."

Oh, for fuck's sake... "What do you want?"

"You assisted Mr. Dante leaving the country, and also leaving a tidy debt behind."

"That's not my business." He rolled his eyes at Mark, who was staring at him with concern.

"It is very much your business, Mr. Ericson. You aided and abetted a felon fleeing the country."

"Oh, so you represent the police?" Evan asked with a sarcastic edge to his voice.

"No, I represent the men from whom Mr. Dante borrowed several thousands of dollars. Unsurprisingly, he has not even attempted to pay any of it back. So, it would seem only reasonable, as you are the one who helped Mr. Dante escape his debt, that you now take responsibility for it."

Evan snorted. "You must be kidding."

"I am not kidding, Mr. Ericson, I am deadly serious. And to show you just how serious, listen to me carefully. You are in a relationship with a Mr. Mark Henderson, yes?"

A shiver ran down Evan's spine and he flicked a nervous glance at Mark. "Mark Henderson and I are working on a movie together. That is the extent of our relationship."

The laughter at the other end of the line was chilling. "Then the photograph I have in front of me of two men walking hand in hand is not of you and Mr. Henderson?"

"We are friends...colleagues really. We were just kidding with the hand holding."

"Oh, I see. So, Mr. Henderson meeting a nasty accident will not concern you overly much?"

"What's going on?" Mark asked, his brow furrowed with concern.

Evan held a finger to his lips to shush him. "Of course I would be extremely upset if anything happened to any friend of mine, but I think this conversation needs to take place in a police station. I will not be threatened or blackmailed, Mr. Whatever Your Name Is. Dareck's business with you is just that—his business, nothing to do with me. And just for the record, I do not have several thousands of dollars at my disposal, so you're looking at the wrong person for recompense. Sorry." He ended the call.

"What the hell was all that?" Mark demanded.

"Some asshole wanting me to pay Dareck's debt. What a joke."

"But I heard you mention my name. Does he want me to pay it? He's fresh outta luck on that score too."

"He's all talk, trying to play the heavy." Evan was not about to relay his fear of himself and Mark being beaten up by hoodlums. He'd just have to be on his toes and make sure Mark wasn't left on his own. He'd also pull in a little backup—not so little, really. Dave Franklin, a cop he'd dated for a couple of months three years ago and kept in touch with from time to time, might be the one to call. He'd know if this was a serious threat or something Evan could safely ignore. After all, whoever had lent Dareck the money had to find some way of collecting, and threats often worked in their favor. But not this time. Besides, he really didn't have that kind of money. Several *thousands*? What the hell was that, and what had Dareck done with it? It couldn't have all gone up his nose.

"You're thinking too hard," Mark said. "That call has got you really worried, hasn't it?"

"Yeah, I wasn't going to tell you about it, but it's better you know so you can keep your guard up. He threatened us, so for the next few days at least, we should stick together like glue. Where you go, I go, okay?" He scrolled through the numbers on his phone until he found the one he wanted. "I'm gonna talk to a cop I know, see if he can help."

"But we don't even know who the guy is that called."

"True, but he's bound to show himself at some point and Dave, the cop I know, might have some ideas on how to deal with that." The call he made went to voicemail, so he left a message asking Dave to get back to him soon as he could. Evan pulled Mark into his arms. "Don't worry, I'm not about to let anything happen to you."

"Shit, how to ruin a day," Mark grumbled, his cheek pressed to Evan's.

"Let's go get something to eat and then decide what we're going to do to keep ourselves safe."

* * * *

"I think you should move in with me until this blows over," Evan said as they walked from the studio to the corner café. "Or maybe even permanently, what d'you think?"

"Wow. I hadn't thought about us moving in together so soon."

"Having second thoughts?"

"God, no." He reached for Evan's hand and held it tight. "I just figured we'd talk about that kind of thing after the movie's completed."

"We can do that." He turned to smile at Mark. "But for right now, it'd be good if we're watching each other's backs, right?"

Mark nodded, but anything he was going to say was stalled when Evan's cell rang. They had reached the café but paused outside while Evan took the call.

"It's Dave," Evan muttered. "Hi, Dave, how's it going?"

"Okay. How 'bout you?" Dave's gruff voice sounded reassuring. "I saw somewhere you're makin' a movie. Good for you."

"Thanks, yeah, it's exciting. Listen, Dave, I have a problem with some loan shark threatening me. Anything you can do to help?"

"You owe a loan shark? What were you thinking?"

"No, I don't owe the guy anything. A friend does, but he's left the country and now this creep wants me to make good the debt because I gave my friend the money to go home."

"I see. You have a name for this guy?"

"No, he never said when he called."

"But you have his number, right? It'll be stored in your phone."

"Oh, duh. Never thought of that."

"Let me have it."

Evan quickly scrolled to recent calls then recited the number to Dave.

"I'll check it against numbers in our database, see what we're dealing with here. I'll call you soon as I have anything — and Evan, be careful."

"Will do. Thanks for your help, Dave." He smiled at Mark. "That makes me feel better. He's gonna check this guy out and get back to me."

There was a short line waiting for tables when they entered the diner.

Mark nudged Evan's hand. "Look over there."

Troy and Gregory were sitting in a booth at the far end of the café. "Didn't know they were buddies."

"They might have just bumped into each other," Evan said, waving in their direction.

Troy said something to Gregory, who looked around at them, then both men got up out of the booth.

"It would appear that we've spoiled their *tête-à-tête*," Evan muttered out of the side of his mouth. "Hi, guys."

Troy smirked. "All through with the shoot?"

"Yep, and it went great," Evan told him.

"I bet." There was no missing the sarcastic tone in Troy's voice.

"You have some kind of problem, Troy?" Evan asked. "Something you want to say?"

Gregory cleared his throat loudly. "We're just on our way to the studio. We'll see you later, perhaps?"

"Yeah, you will. You and I have a scene together, and you too, Troy." Evan was pissed at the guy's stupid attitude. He turned at the touch of Mark's hand on his arm.

"Don't get upset. There's enough going on without letting

asshole Troy get under your skin."

Evan sighed. "You're right." He smiled brightly at the young hostess, who was staring at him as if mesmerized. "Table for two?"

"Oh, yes, sir." She kept staring at Evan, then Mark, then back again at Evan. "This way please, sirs." She handed them menus as they settled in the booth then asked if they'd like anything to drink.

"Ice-cold beer, please. Stella, if you have it. Mark?"

"Same for me, thanks."

She beamed at them and fluttered her eyelashes. "I'll get those right now for you."

Evan watched her hurry away and grinned at Mark. "I think I'm going to like going everywhere with you. I get the best service when we're together."

"Ha!" Mark snorted. "Methinks it's the other way 'round."

Evan's expression grew serious and he drummed his fingers on the table in irritation. "You think I should tell Charles and Richard about this guy threatening us? Damn, I could kick myself for getting you involved. I should've told Dareck to take a hike."

Mark shook his head. "No, you shouldn't have—and you wouldn't, you're too nice a guy to let a friend down, so don't start blaming yourself for everything. It's just like that old saying—no good deed goes unpunished. We have to ride this out, that's all, and if your friend the cop can maybe intervene, that'd be great. I don't know about telling Charles and Richard. They have a lot on their minds right now."

"You're right…" He paused as the hostess came back with their drinks and another sunny smile.

"I'll send Margie right over to take your order."

"Thank you." Evan took a long pull on his beer, opened the menu and stared at it in silence for a few minutes, then put it down again. "Don't think I'm hungry after all."

"Evan…" Mark reached across the table and took his hand. "You are going to be in the studio for hours, possibly.

You really should have something to eat. I don't want to sound like your mother but…"

"You could never sound like my mother, and you're right, I'm being juvenile."

"I didn't say that."

"I know, I said it. Okay, I'll have turkey on rye. What about you?"

"Cheeseburger, I think. Yeah, that'll do it."

"Hi, I'm Margie." They both glanced up at the sweet-faced young girl smiling down at them. "I'll be taking care of you today."

"That's nice," Mark said.

"Have you decided?"

"Yes, turkey on rye for me, and my boyfriend will have a cheeseburger," Evan told her.

"Oh, I said to Lorraine you guys are gay. You're too good-looking to be straight."

"Aw, that's sweet of you, though there are some good-looking straight guys out there."

"Yes, but they're usually stuck-up and full of themselves. Not like you. You're both so friendly, even though you are *really* handsome." Margie blushed and Evan chuckled.

"You have that in common with Mark, here. See? He's blushing too."

Margie joined in the laughter then seemed to remember she was working. "Oh, what about sides?"

"I try not to take them," Evan deadpanned.

"Oh, you have your choice of fries, coleslaw, onion rings…" Margie went on, oblivious to Evan's attempt at humor.

"Fries for me," Mark said.

"And me."

Margie gave them another big smile and left.

"'I try not to take them'," Mark scoffed.

"Hey, I thought that was pretty funny. Just trying to lighten the mood of the day. Mark, have you ever wondered what it would be like to have an ordinary, uneventful life? Take each day as it comes, not worry about stuff. Like Margie... work in a restaurant, smile at customers..."

"Work for minimum wage, smile at customers when they're being assholes. Yeah, Evan..." Mark snorted. "Been there, done that, don't want to do it again."

"Whoa, sorry. I obviously touched a nerve there. I guess I was being silly talking that way."

"You do know that Margie might want to jump at the chance of being a model or working in movies, right?" Mark continued, still sounding slightly annoyed. "Being a food server is a necessary and respectable job, but it brings its own share of worries, like not making enough on tips to feed the kids. That kind of stuff. I worked with people like that, trying hard to make ends meet."

"Mark, I said I'm sorry. You're right. Apart from having to put up with shitty foster parents when I was a kid, I've had it good in my life, and I should appreciate it more than I do." He smiled. "Kinda hot to see you get all fired up, though."

Mark sighed. "I'm sorry too. It's just that I have been poor. Before I got this job, I couldn't even afford to go *see* a movie. I was trying to find another job waiting tables... but that's enough of that." His expression lightened and he grinned. "How hot?"

Evan opened his mouth to tell him, but just then his cell chimed and he grabbed it off the tabletop. "Evan Ericson."

"Yeah, hi Evan, it's Dave. Hate to say this, but you've got yourself mixed up with a nasty bunch. Miguel Castro is the man who called you. He runs a drug trafficking syndicate here in LA. He's been up on charges multiple times, beats them at every turn with the help of a high-powered attorney. He has spent less time in jail than a petty criminal. We've been watching him for months trying to get some solid evidence against him, but no one will talk to us."

"This doesn't sound good, Dave."

"It's not. You and your friend are going to have to be careful. I'll talk to the chief and see if I can arrange some kind of protection for you. Where is the movie you're making being filmed?"

"Uh, Woodside Studios on Burbank. I'm going back there in about a half hour."

"And do you still live on Robertson?"

"Yes."

"Do you know how much the friend you helped owed Castro?"

"No. Only that he said several thousand dollars."

"Which probably means close to at least twenty-five grand."

"Jesus."

"Yeah, they wouldn't bother with you if it was, oh, around five or so."

"So, what do we do now? Wait for him to contact me again? You think it might be possible to bargain with him?" At this point, Evan was willing to find any kind of solution in order to protect Mark. He'd seen the effects of beatings by drug dealers on those who didn't pay up, and the thought of Mark's beautiful face being ruined by thugs made his blood run cold.

"Leave it with me for a day or so," Dave said. "I have a connection that might be able to get a message to Castro. In the meantime, I'll see if I can arrange for someone to keep an eye on you."

"Thanks, Dave. I owe you."

Dave chuckled. "Well, we'll talk about that some other time. Just be careful."

Margie took that moment to drop their food off. Evan stared at his plate and said, "Now I'm really not hungry."

"Margie..." Mark smiled at her. "You think we could have a couple of to-go bags?"

* * * *

When they got back to the studio they exchanged worried glances as sounds of a disturbance reached them out in the corridor. "What the hell?" Evan pushed the door open and the din increased. Charles and Troy were standing on set raging at each other while Gregory stood off to one side looking worried. Roger, Richard and the crew were scattered about, some attending to business, others blatantly watching the drama.

"What's going on?" Mark asked Roger.

The cameraman's expression was grim. "We went for a take," he said, his voice low. "Charles didn't like the way Troy was fluffing his lines and missing his marks, which is understandable. We're on a tight schedule here, as you know. Troy threw a hissy fit, blamed the script, said the way it was written it was hard to remember — which is bullshit, of course. No one else has had that problem. So, the two of them went at it, and still are, as you can see and hear." Roger shook his head. "Charles is gonna can the little shit if he keeps this up."

"But aren't they…uh…?" Mark was unsure how much Roger would know about Charles' and Troy's involvement.

"Won't matter. Charles won't put up with this for much longer."

As if to prove what Roger had just said, Troy, his face scarlet with rage, stormed off the set shouting threats of repercussions over his shoulder at Charles. When he saw Evan and Mark standing with Roger his face flushed an even darker shade of red.

"And you, you pair of amateurs," he screamed at them, "you'll be the ruination of this film, and he can't see it. You're disgusting, swooning over each other in front of us every day."

Mark felt Evan tense beside him and he gripped his arm in case he had thoughts of slugging Troy.

"You'll never get to work on any other movie, I'll make sure of that." Troy pointed at Charles. "That son of a bitch just fired me, and — "

"Get out, Troy!" Charles yelled. "Go to the apartment, pack your things and be gone by the time I get there."

Mark could not believe what was unfolding in front of him and everyone in the studio. Claire and Pamela stood off to one side, their faces pale with concern as they watched the two men rage at each other. How much more drama could there be in one day? A deathly hush fell over the studio after Troy slammed the door behind him.

Richard was the first to speak. He cleared his throat, "Everyone, take ten, then we'll convene here for a short meeting." He beckoned Mark and Evan over. "Charles has gone to the back office to calm down. Sorry you had to see all that. We'll be apologizing to everyone else when we meet."

"Is Troy going to stay fired?" Evan asked. "I imagine he'd have a hard time facing everyone again after that tirade."

"He and Charles are through. It's been coming for some time and Charles has been increasingly frustrated with Troy's poor performance. He just won't listen to Charles' advice."

"Which makes him all kinds of a fool, in my opinion," Evan said. "Charles is one of the most respected directors in the industry. He could've learned so much from him."

Richard nodded. "And one of the most generous. Young Troy is going to find life without Charles a little hard to bear." He shrugged. "But that's his problem. Our problem will be finding a replacement for him at this stage, and we'll have to recall Marsha, but we'll tackle that after the meeting."

Charles walked toward them, looking pale but composed. Mark wanted to give him a hug but wondered if that would be inappropriate at that moment. Evan obviously had no such qualms as he wrapped Charles in his arms and held him in a comforting embrace.

"You'll make me sob if you keep that up, Evan," Charles said, his voice sounding as if it was on the verge of breaking. "But I appreciate it. Richard, get everyone in here. It's time to move on with our project. My own personal feelings can be put on the back burner for the time being."

The crew had already begun to filter back into the studio and Charles wasted no time in calling them together. "First, I want to apologize to all of you for that unbelievably unprofessional scene between Troy and myself. It was inevitable, but also unforgiveable, and I do apologize from the bottom of my heart. Of course, this will cause us to redo some scenes, and because of our limited budget and time frame we must attend to that immediately. We're a month into filming and I will need all of you to muck in and give me as many extra hours in the day as possible. You will of course be recompensed under union guidelines. So now, I ask that we get on with it. Evan and Gregory, your scene will be shot next. Thank you."

He walked over to his director's chair while the crew scrambled to set the scene. Evan went to Wardrobe, and Roger and Tim cued up the cameras. Finally, Frank called, "Places," and everything proceeded as if there had never been an altercation between director and actor. Mark sat on the sidelines watching Evan and Gregory enact the detective's first interrogation of the murdered woman's friends, or in Gregory's case, enemy. The scene was intense, Gregory, as Clark Cooper, very much on the defensive and Evan relentless in his questioning. When Charles called "Cut!" he looked pleased, and after some conversation with Evan and Gregory, there was a second take then a wrap.

Evan's next scene was to have been with Troy, and it was then that Mark remembered Brett Lester's phone call. He had intended to get in touch with him, but as the weeks had passed so full of the movie — and Evan — his good intentions had been sorely lacking. He hadn't even called Kyle in several days. He hurried over to where Richard and Charles were in deep conversation.

"Uh...sorry, don't mean to interrupt," he said as the two men turned to look at him, "but if you want someone to replace Troy, you might consider Brett Lester, Ron Lester's son. He actually wanted to audition for the role you gave me, but apparently his dad wouldn't allow it."

Richard stared at him. "Why not?"

Mark shrugged. "Something about wanting to keep him in the office."

"Does he have experience?" Charles asked.

"He said he's taken acting classes, done some amateur stuff. He may not be what you're looking for, but I bet he'd jump at the chance to audition for you."

"Call him," Charles said, "and tell him if he's interested to get over here this afternoon, if he can. I'll talk to Ron Lester if the boy is any good."

Mark felt a guilty pang as he realized he hadn't even mentioned Perry or Andrew for the role. Perry was wrong physically, and perhaps a bit too mature to play a boy-toy — and Andrew, maybe too effeminate? *Shit, he really shouldn't be making these judgment calls.* If Charles and Richard weren't impressed with Brett, he could give them his roommates' names instead. He put the call in to Brett, who sounded so excited at the possibility of working on the movie, Mark thought the guy might just leap tall buildings to get to the studio that afternoon.

"I'll tell Pop that I'm taking the rest of the afternoon off. See you there!"

He went to find Evan and suggested he go home to pick up some changes of clothes for the time he was going to spend at Evan's apartment.

Evan grabbed his arm and uttered a resounding, "No! You're not going anywhere without me, Mark. I thought we'd decided on that. Safety in numbers, remember? When I'm through here we will both go to your apartment so you can pack some stuff, then we'll head over to my place. No going anywhere on your own."

"Okay, boss," Mark said meekly.

"Good boy." Evan grinned at him. "Hey, I think I got my appetite back. What did you do with those sandwiches?"

Chapter Nine

Brett arrived within half an hour, and after Mark introduced him to Richard and Charles he was taken into the office to audition. Mark knew nothing about Brett's acting skills or lack of same, but from Mark's perspective, Brett's personality alone had already charmed the director. An hour later Brett was led out onto the set and Roger went to work filming him while he read lines, walked around and sat at the desk that had been left on set. He looked like a natural to Mark, and even more so when Charles directed him in a scene with Evan. Everything was happening at lightning speed, and Mark couldn't help but wonder what would happen if, when Charles got home, Troy was there on his knees, asking for forgiveness and begging to be reinstated in the movie.

"I think we're going to try a take with Brett and Evan," Charles said later. "Don't worry, Brett," he added on seeing the flare of panic in the young man's eyes, "we know you'll need the script, but in this scene Evan does most of the talking. Just react to what he's saying. He's suspicious of you, trying to link you to the murder..."

They ran the scene, and when they watched the playback, it was obvious Brett was good. He even had Evan pinned with a smoldering look in his eyes as Evan got into his personal space with a hard question.

"Cut! Great!' Charles yelled. "Okay, Brett, go with Pamela, she'll help you with the lines. We'll shoot this scene tomorrow and I'll get Marsha here for her scene with you. That was excellent, Brett. And, Evan, thanks for what you did there."

Mark could see Brett's excitement bubbling up inside him.

"I'll call your father," Charles said. "Get him to see the light, okay? I'll have a contract ready for you before you leave."

Brett threw his arms around Mark. "Thanks so much for doing this for me. I can't believe I'm going to be a part of this!" He kissed Mark full on the lips and Evan growled.

"Oh, sorry. Are you two...?" Brett looked away in embarrassment.

Mark laughed. "That's okay, Brett. Evan's not the jealous kind. Are you, Evan?"

"Not at all," Evan replied with an innocent expression. "Totally not the jealous kind. Way too mature for that."

"Well, thank you both," Brett said, regaining his composure. "I guess I'll see you tomorrow."

"You will. Goodnight."

Evan put an arm around Mark's shoulders as they walked to the exit. Mark turned to look at him and smirked.

"Possessive, much?"

"Just stakin' my claim so he knows what's what." He dropped his arm to encircle Mark's waist and pulled him close. "Okay now, when we leave here, be on the lookout for any suspicious characters. Dave said he was going to try to have one of his guys on our tails, but just in case it hasn't happened yet, we need to be alert."

"You really think they'd try to beat us up?"

"Well, that Castro guy sounded pretty serious, and I have seen the results of drug dealer punishment. So we just have to be careful until I hear from Dave again."

They stepped outside into the dimly lit parking lot and stood for a moment or two, scanning the rows of parked cars. It did seem like a good place for an ambush, Mark had to admit. He kept close to Evan as they made their way to his car. Fortunately, they were parked side by side, so when Mark slid into his car, Evan said, "I'll follow you, okay? Keep an eye out for anyone behind us that shouldn't be."

Not an easy task on Burbank and West Hollywood's busy

streets, he thought as he watched Evan get into his car. He was slightly on edge the entire way to his apartment, but it didn't appear they had been followed. At least not as far as Mark could tell. *But you're no expert on all things sleuthing, or whatever they call this…* After he pulled into his designated spot, he waited for Evan on the sidewalk while he searched for somewhere to leave his car. He got a little edgy as the minutes crept past and almost jumped out of his skin when a heavy hand landed on his shoulder and a voice behind him drawled, "Out soliciting again?"

"Perry! Jeez, you scared me."

"Guilty conscience? Or are you really a hooker?"

"Funny guy. I'm waiting for Evan to park his car."

"Good luck with that around here. Oh wait. This divine vision coming our way must be he. Stellar looks guarantee you a parking space, as well as everything else in the world, it seems."

"You're in a jovial mood tonight," Mark said.

"Yes." He held out his hand as Evan joined them. "You must be the Evan we've been hearing so much about."

"Evan, this is Perry, one of my roommates."

"The only one worth mentioning, of course."

Evan chuckled and shook Perry's hand. "Nice to meet you."

"Nice to eat—I mean meet you too."

Mark rolled his eyes. Perry's personality veered between being a sarcastic twit or, on occasion, a second-rate comedian. Or as he himself called it, end-of-the-pier humor.

"So, to what do we owe the pleasure of your company?" Perry asked as they stepped into the apartment building's elevator.

"Uh, we're picking up some of my stuff," Mark told him. "I'll be staying with Evan for a couple of days."

"Oh, nice. Not seeing enough of each other during filming hours?"

"Something like that, yeah." There was just a trace of annoyance edging Evan's voice, but Perry must have heard it loud and clear because he immediately backed off from the needling.

"Well, I think that is splendid. Will you have a drink with us before you go?"

Mark hesitated and Evan said, "Thanks, but we need to get a move on. Another time?"

"Of course." They got off the elevator and Mark practically hustled Evan to their apartment door.

"You can help me pack." He continued the hustling through the living room and into his bedroom. "Sorry, but if you stay out there with Perry we'll never get out of here."

"He is a character."

"And a half." Mark pulled a suitcase from the closet and began throwing underwear, socks, T-shirts and jeans into it. "Don't think I'll need anything formal, do you?"

"Only when I take you to the ball." Evan grinned at him and put his arms around Mark's waist. "That bed looks mighty enticing, but Perry being out there kinda kills the moment."

"You're telling me. Let's go. You can have your way with me when we get to your place."

* * * *

When they got into Evan's car, he slipped his cell into the Bluetooth slot. "Just in case Dave tries to get a hold of me."

There was no call from Dave, nor was there any sign of them being followed, and Mark relaxed considerably once inside Evan's apartment. Unlike the one Mark shared with Perry and Andrew, Evan's building had a secured entry and garage, and a concierge on duty twenty-four-seven.

"Bring your case through to the bedroom. I'll find a drawer for your undies and socks, or you can stick them in with mine, all nice and cozy."

Mark chuckled. "I'm sure they'll feel right at home next to your undies."

"I like this already."

"What's that?"

"You and me, together, in one place."

Evan slid his hands under Mark's T-shirt and teased both nipples with his thumbs. Mark sighed happily and met Evan's mouth with a ready kiss, opening for Evan's tongue, savoring the sensation of it gliding over his. He was hard in an instant and, from the feel of what was pressing against his crotch, Evan was right there with him. Mark raised his arms and Evan slipped off his T-shirt, then followed by hauling off his own. Their bare chests slapped together as they embraced again and Mark shivered from the sensuous touch of skin on skin.

"Think it's bedtime," Evan murmured. "Wanna see you all stretched out under me, naked, that beautiful body of yours completely mine to do with what I will."

"Mmm… You'll get no argument from me on that score."

Wasting no time, they hurried into the bedroom. In the light cast by the bedside lamps Evan's eyes gleamed with desire. He leaned in for a kiss and Mark parted his lips to take Evan's exploring tongue. With one hand he cupped the back of Mark's neck, holding him into the kiss, while with the other he unsnapped the button at the waistband of Mark's jeans and pulled the zipper down. Mark sat on the edge of the bed and let Evan deftly remove his shoes, socks and jeans then quickly discard his own.

As Evan climbed on top of him, Mark whispered, "Need you under me. Let me lick every part of the body that drives me crazy just by looking at it."

Evan's eyes widened in surprise for just a moment, then he rolled onto his back with a sigh of agreement and what sounded like anticipation. Evan's erect cock curved against his stomach and Mark took a moment to simply admire its proud beauty. Then Mark straddled him, taking his wrists in his hands and pinning him to the mattress. Their gazes locked, and Evan's lips quirked with a kind of 'what now?' expression. Mark covered his mouth with a long, hard kiss then stretched himself over Evan, pressing their heated bodies together. He licked his way from Evan's mouth, over his throat, into each armpit, inhaling Evan's masculine scent. Evan moaned and bucked under Mark but didn't try to break free of Mark's pin. Mark had to release him to reach the other parts he wanted to lick and nibble on…but first, he eased Evan onto his stomach and ran his tongue down the length of Evan's spine to the cleft between his butt cheeks.

Evan let out a deep groan of pleasure and writhed under him as Mark teased the puckered opening with the tip of his tongue. He palmed each cheek, parting them to give himself greater access. He pushed in, burying his face between the warm twin globes of smooth, muscular flesh. He'd been longing to do this for Evan ever since Evan had proven to him just how incredible and completely intimate it could be. For some reason, probably because he became totally lost in whatever Evan did to him and was content to let him take the lead, this was the first time he had gotten this far. He hoped he was doing a good job, and if Evan's soft moans and whimpers were anything to go by, he was. He added a finger, using his saliva as lubricant, reaching in to stroke the sensitive gland inside Evan's tight passage.

Evan raised his hips to take all of Mark's finger inside. "Fuck me," Evan murmured. "You've taken me this far, now I need your cock all the way inside me…"

"Need that too, lover." Mark reached for the drawer where Evan kept the lube and condoms. Evan turned to lie on his back, smiling up at Mark.

"Here, let me put it on you." Evan ripped the foil wrapper with his teeth then gave Mark a salacious grin. "C'mere…"

Mark watched with fascination as Evan put the condom between his lips then slipped it over Mark's cock using only the gliding motion of his lips. Mark didn't think it was possible to get any harder than he already was, but from the way Evan's beautiful lust-filled eyes were mesmerizing him at that moment, it certainly felt as if he did.

He poured the lube onto his fingers and got Evan ready,

stretching him the way Evan had for him. He guided his now aching cock between Evan's thighs and pushed slowly forward. Evan gasped as the broad head of Mark's shaft eased into him. He raised himself up and wrapped his arms around Mark's torso, holding him steady while he seated himself onto Mark's lap. With one quick downward plunge he took all of Mark's throbbing dick inside him. Mark watched his lover's face for traces of pain, relieved when Evan's lips parted, his head fell back and he uttered what could only be described as a long moan of unadulterated satisfaction.

"Feels so good, Mark."

"Feels fantastic."

Mark bucked his hips, driving himself deeper into Evan's tight heat, and Evan pushed down to take him all the way in. With their arms about each other in a fierce embrace, their mouths and bodies fused together, they began a slow, intense rhythm that wrung moans of ecstasy out of them both. Mark was in heaven. The thrilling sensation of Evan's smooth, muscular body under his hands sent jolts of exquisite pleasure through his blood. Being inside him, being a part of him, inhaling the scent of his hair, his sweat, his very essence, all of it he was going to store away in his mind and keep for times when they might be apart. He knew he would remember these sensations forever.

"Oh, God, Mark…"

Evan's soft lips vibrating on his sent a visceral thrill through every nerve in Mark's body. Evan fell back onto the mattress, pulling Mark with him, deepening the kiss that had started out as tender and sweet and now morphed into an almost feverish union of lips, teeth and tongues.

Caught up in the passion that seemed to spill from their very pores, Mark drove himself into his lover with powerful thrusts of his pelvis, their sweat-slicked bodies sliding over each other, the press of flesh on flesh dizzying in its intensity. Mark looked down at his lover's face, caught in the rapture of near-orgasm, and his heart leaped in his chest. He gripped Evan's erection, loving the feel of the pulsing hardness in his hand, pumping it with long, urgent strokes.

"Aaah…" Evan's cry of release came as he thrashed like a bucking bronco under Mark, his hot semen splashing onto his heaving chest. His eyes flew open and he pulled Mark in for another kiss that sent Mark's senses spiraling out of control, into the void of a climax he was sure caused him to black out for several seconds. A low groan of sheer ecstasy was torn from him. His shuddering body spasmed uncontrollably, and he emptied himself into Evan's depths.

"Jesus…" Mark rested his sweating forehead on Evan's. His panting breath slowly calmed and the fog in his brain cleared.

Evan chuckled and wiped the sweat from Mark's brow with his fingers. "My thoughts exactly. I know I have never been so royally fucked in my life — and I mean that in only the best possible way." He licked Mark's sweat from his fingers. "Mmm, salty and sweet, just like the rest of you."

"I love you," Mark whispered.

"Love you too…" He clenched his ass muscles around the base of Mark's cock. "Mmm… Stay inside me for the rest of the night."

"Wish I could."

"You could. I think I feel you gettin' hard again."

Mark chuckled and snuggled down at Evan's side. "Dream on…"

Chapter Ten

They were wakened early next morning by the insistent chiming of Evan's cell phone. "Who the hell?" he muttered, straining to see the clock by his bed. "Six — shit." He peered at the ID screen. *Dave...* "Hi, Dave. You're up and about early."

"No, just the opposite. I'm just clocking off and going home."

"Oh, yeah. Graveyard shift, huh?" He smiled at Mark, who was sitting up, rubbing his eyes and looking totally fuckable. He got distracted for a moment by the sight of Mark's perky ass when he rolled out of bed and headed for the bathroom.

"Right. Anyway, I got a message from my Castro contact and he says your Hungarian friend — he knew exactly who I was talking about, by the way — owed Castro fifty grand."

"What? Holy shit. What the hell would he want with that amount of money?"

"Sending it home to his mama, Evan. You got suckered."

"That little...twerp."

"Yep. He told Castro his mother needed surgery and he'd pay every cent back by getting off the drugs and working hard. I'm kinda surprised they went for it, but these guys have ways of getting their money back, if only by monthly payments. I guess they didn't expect him to skip out of the country. The way they see it, your little friend managed to leave with your help, and now they want you to cough it up."

"Fifty grand? You know I don't have that kind of money, Dave." *Oh, this is already starting out to be a really crappy day.*

The days of him earning big bucks from modeling were gone.

"Didn't think you did, but they're not willing to negotiate the amount, I'm sorry to say."

"So, what do I do?"

"Run like hell."

"What?"

"Just kidding. Look, I've talked to the chief and he agrees with me. This is an opportunity for us to get him and his guys off the street—with your help."

"*My* help?"

"Yep, but I don't want to discuss this over the phone. Where can I meet you today?"

"I'll be at the studio all day. We're close to wrapping up the production and I have to be there. What if I call you when we take a break?"

"That'll work. I have someone keeping an eye on you, by the way, so you'll be okay till we figure out how we get this done."

"Thanks, Dave." Evan didn't like the sound of 'get this done', but if it meant keeping Mark safe and not having to find fifty grand to pay off Dareck's debt, he was up for it.

"What was that all about?" Mark asked, getting back into bed.

"Dave's trying to figure out a way to get that Castro guy off my back." He was glad Mark hadn't heard the whole conversation. No point in worrying him until he heard what Dave had planned.

Mark snuggled into Evan's side and kissed his neck. "Did he say how he's gonna do that?"

"He's working on it. I have to call him when we take a break today." He just hoped that whatever it was, it could be taken care of quickly.

* * * *

Marsha seemed pleased to see them when they arrived at

Woodside Studios. "I thought I wouldn't see you two till post-production, and only if they needed us for reshoots." She gave each of them a hug. "And I like Troy's replacement. Much easier to get along with than that spoiled brat. Did you hear what happened?"

Mark was amused by Marsha's eagerness to spill the beans. "You mean after Charles canned him and he stormed outta here the other day?"

"Yes, after." Marsha looked around as if to make sure no one was listening. "Poor Charles. He had to call the cops. Troy had destroyed the apartment, and Charles had some really priceless antiques in there. Can you believe that nasty kid would do such a thing?"

Mark didn't find it hard to believe it, but he felt sorry for Charles. Like making a movie wasn't stressful enough.

"He's got insurance, of course," Marsha said, "but some of that stuff is irreplaceable, and lots of memories are wrapped up in it. If that little fucker ever shows his face near me I will delight in slapping it so hard he'll need a jaw replacement."

Both Mark and Evan snorted out surprised laughs at Marsha's choice of words. "Wow, remind me never to get on your bad side, Marsha," Evan said, still laughing.

Marsha laughed too, but Mark could tell by the glint in her eye that she hadn't been kidding. "Did he have Troy arrested?"

"No, but they are through. My guess is Troy is winging his way back to Bumfuck, Montana, where he belongs."

Evan chuckled. "Bad luck for Bumfuck, Montana."

Gregory joined them, looking morose. "I should explain something to you so you don't get the wrong idea about Troy and myself."

"Is there a wrong idea?" Evan asked, grinning.

"No, no... I knew you were probably curious as to why Troy and I were in the diner together the other day. I can assure you, it was totally innocent, on my part anyway."

"You, innocent?" Marsha chortled. "There isn't an

innocent bone in that lecherous old body of yours." She peered at him, narrowing her eyes. "What were you up to?"

"Nothing, and it's none of your business. I was talking to Evan and Mark."

Marsha folded her arms across her chest. "Hmpf… Be careful, Greg. Charles won't like to hear that you and his ex were in cahoots."

"We were not in cahoots, as you so eloquently put it. Oh, for heaven's sake, the boy wanted some acting advice, is all. He was worried that Charles was displeased and—"

"And he was right!" Marsha exclaimed.

"He didn't really go about it sensibly," Evan remarked. "I can understand him coming to you for advice, Gregory, but to stand there railing at the director is the dumbest thing he could've done."

Gregory sighed. "That might have been my fault. I told him he was working with one of the best directors in the industry and—"

"And sleeping with him," Marsha interrupted.

"Marsha! Would you please stop?" Gregory clenched and unclenched his hands in frustration. "I told Troy to speak honestly with Charles and ask him for help with how he wanted to portray his character."

"And it deteriorated into a bitch-fest because Troy could never be told what to do or how to conduct himself." Marsha smirked. "I for one am not unhappy to see him go. Brett is a much nicer boy, and so willing to learn."

"Gregory, we really didn't think you and Troy were up to no good," Evan told the older actor.

"You're too nice a guy to have anything to do with Troy," Mark added.

"Well, thank you." Gregory ignored Marsha's snort. "I just wanted to clear the air between us."

"And you have," Evan said. "It's all good."

Charles called for Evan and Gregory at that moment, and the business of making a movie continued.

* * * *

Mark took advantage of some time to himself to call Kyle. They hadn't talked in almost two weeks — Mark's fault for not responding to Kyle's voicemail messages. He knew there was no emergency. Kyle had sounded as chirpy as usual, but he didn't want them to lose touch.

"Hi, Kyle," he said when his friend answered.

"Oh, my God, it's the movie star finally deigning to speak to the peon."

"Shut up. Sorry, it's been kinda hectic. We really need to get together soon. I want you to meet Evan."

"Aha! I smell a romance. Tell me everything."

"Not everything, but yes, we're in a relationship...and it's great. Terrific really. How about you and Josh?"

"Oh, we're just plodding along — fucking every night. The man is insatiable — *insatiable*, I tell you! Who knew that Mr. Josh Button-down Marks would be such a horndog? Oh, my poor aching butthole!"

Mark laughed. "TMI, Kyle, definitely TMI."

"Oh, come on. Who else can I tell my sexual exploits to?" He sighed loudly. "He is just *mahvellous*. So, you're in heat, but how's the movie going?"

"Great. A few dramas, but we're getting there. The director figures we'll be in post-production in a couple of weeks."

"Post-production. Words I knew I'd hear you say one day. Hey, that rhymes. So you're well, happy, getting laid?"

"All of the above."

Kyle screeched and Mark jerked the phone away from his ear. "I am so happy for you...and me...and Josh...and whatsisname."

"Evan."

"Right, Evan. I can't wait to meet him, and see the movie and the two of you doing it on the big screen."

"Kyle..." Mark chuckled. "You are too much. We don't really do it."

"No? I just read on the Internet about couples who've actually done it during a sex scene."

"That's called porn."

"No no…these were real actors. They just got carried away, I guess."

"Well, I have to admit I can see how it could happen, but not in this instance. Just simulated, I'm afraid."

"Darn. Well, have to go, Joe. Another dreary day at work looms ahead. The only bright spot is when Josh and I get home and I get ready."

"I'm afraid to ask for what."

"Exactly what your dirty mind has dredged up. Your best friend will be ass up in bed waiting to be fertilized."

"Oh, my God! I just had to bleach that visual from my memory banks. Bye, Kyle." He shook his head as his friend's cackle faded away. *Well, I'm happy for him. He deserves to have someone in his life – even if it is sourpuss Josh.*

* * * *

Evan jerked his head toward the studio door, where the silhouette of a large figure was framed in the doorway. *Dave…let's hope this is good news.* "Hey, Dave." He waved and hurried over to his friend from his modeling days. Tall, broad-shouldered, his dark-brown hair now lightly streaked with gray, Dave Franklin was still an imposing presence. He caught Evan up in a bear hug and kissed him on the forehead.

"You look even better than I remember," he said, holding Evan at arm's-length, his gaze sweeping over Evan's face and body. "Why did I ever let you go?"

Evan laughed. "You were married to your job, if I recall."

"And you were traipsing all over the world. Well, it's good to see you. I'm glad you called me. Where's your friend?"

Looking around, Evan spotted Mark talking to one of the sound techs but watching him and Dave at the same time. "Hey, Mark…when you're done, come meet Dave."

Mark crossed the studio floor and approached them, a nervous expression on his face.

"Dave, this is my boyfriend, Mark Henderson." Evan took Mark's arm and drew him in close. He watched as the men shook hands, and Mark seemed to relax under Dave's broad smile.

"Good to meet you, Mark. Sorry about the circumstances, but chances are I'd never have heard from Evan if there wasn't some kind of problem."

Evan tried not to feel guilty at Dave's words. "We've talked...but you're right, Dave, I'm terrible at keeping in touch, but it's good to see you."

"Is there somewhere we can talk in private?"

Mark gestured at the corridor that led to the break room. "There's no one taking a break right now. We can use the room while it's empty."

"Good enough." Dave followed them as they led the way past the camera and sound equipment. "So, this is where it all happens. I've never seem a movie in progress before."

"You should stay and see Evan in his next scene," Mark said. "We can ask Charles if it's okay that you watch him in action."

"That'd be great."

They entered the break room and sat at one of the tables.

"So, here's the deal." Dave kept his voice low even though they were the only ones in the room. "Castro wants fifty thousand — you don't have it, but you can offer him a helluva lot more."

Evan stared at him in surprise. "I can?"

"Yep. You can offer him fifty thousand dollars' worth of cocaine, which on the street will rake in five, six times as much. And if I'm right about the punk, he'll leap at the chance to acquire that much blow."

"But where the hell would I find that amount of coke?"

Dave grinned. "Oh, we have some lying around. Okay, I've talked with the chief, and with your help we're going to put together a sting operation. This is how it will work. You will call Castro and make the offer. Sound very nervous. You're an actor, so you can do it. Make him believe you managed to acquire the coke by devious means, which of course you cannot divulge to him. He won't question you too much, but he will be suspicious of the quality. He's gonna want to check it out. You will have to meet with him face to face."

Mark shifted uncomfortably. "Won't that be dangerous? Evan alone with a criminal?"

"Don't worry, we'll be there, only Castro can't know about our involvement."

"So, I meet with him, then what?" Evan asked, leaning forward in his seat.

"You'll have a sample for him to check out. You'll wear a wire. Any conversation you have with Castro or his cronies will be picked up by us and recorded as evidence. Don't worry, wires are totally unnoticeable these days. Tiny, like a thread. Once he's okay with the quality, he'll arrange with you a time and place for the drop-off. You will hand the cocaine over, and that's when we step in and arrest him. We figure once he's out of the picture the rest of the cartel will dissolve. There might be somebody there who thinks he can become the kingpin, but that'll be easier for us to deal with. Castro is the one we want, and from what I've heard about the guy, he might just sing about the rest of the thugs he's involved with."

Mark visibly shivered. "It still sounds dangerous to me."

Dave nodded. "There is a danger factor, I won't deny it. These guys are volatile, and Castro will be suspicious. It's up to you, Evan, to come across scared enough to get them off your back. That you'll do anything to be free of the debt. How d'you feel about this?"

Evan chuckled. "Well, I've got the scared part down perfect. I won't have to act too hard to make them believe it."

"Are you sure, Evan?" Mark asked. "About this, I mean? What if these guys are armed?"

"Oh, they will be," Dave said grimly. "They don't go anywhere without guns. So, yeah, there is a distinct possibility there will be a show of arms. But they're not gonna shoot you, Evan. Castro will want the deal, I'm sure of it."

"How sure?" Mark snapped.

"Sure as I am about anything to do with drug dealers. Number one, they are greedy. Money means everything to them, and a deal like this will look mighty sweet to Castro." Dave paused and looked at Evan, a frown creasing his forehead. "Okay, now this has to be entirely your decision, Evan. I'll understand if you don't want to get involved. I won't underestimate the danger aspect of it. All I can do is tell you that we will be with you every step of the way."

"Okay, I'll do it." Evan smiled at Mark and took his hand. "I'm not gonna be on my own, babe. I'll have LA's finest at my back. It'll be fine."

The door swung open at that moment and two of the crew stepped inside. Dave stood and indicated with a jerk of his head that they should leave. Just then his cell phone rang.

"Franklin. Yeah? Okay, be right there. Sorry, guys." He gave Evan and Mark a rueful look. "Have to take a rain check on watching the movie action. Gotta head into the precinct right away."

"That sucks," Evan said. "And here I was ready to show you my acting chops."

Dave grinned. "Next time." Evan and Mark walked him over to the exit. "I'll be in touch once I get the details ironed out with the chief. If Castro calls again, tell him you're working on a deal to get him his money. That'll shut him up for a while."

They said their goodbyes, then Mark dragged Evan into a dark corner of the studio and wrapped his arms around him. "I don't want you to do this, Evan, I really don't. Surely we can work this out without you having to put yourself in danger. We can get a loan, pay this Castro guy off and get on with our lives."

Evan leaned into Mark's embrace and nuzzled his throat. "I think there's more to it than just paying off Dareck's debt. What Dave is trying to do is put some bad guys out of business, and I'm all for that. A year and half ago I gave up drugs. It was tough. I wasn't exactly an addict, but I came pretty close, and I saw, because of the company I kept, some really bad scenes. Guys strung out so bad they had to be taken to the ER. Some didn't make it. During that time I had unprotected sex with men, and sometimes I had no clue who they even were. I was lucky. At the end of it all I was clear of STDs. I was broke, but I still considered myself lucky. I don't judge people who get off on drugs, but a part of me wants to see guys like Miguel Castro shut down, put away for a nice long stretch, and the drugs he sells just that little bit harder to get."

"So, this is like a crusade?" Mark frowned at him. "You want to put your life in danger in order to stop one drug dealer when there are a hundred more like him out there ready to take over his business? What about me, Evan? What about *us*? If anything happened to you now, I just don't know what I'd do…"

"Nothing's gonna happen to me, babe. Okay, I wasn't going to admit this to you…" He caressed Mark's face with is fingertips. His voice was low and rueful, although his gaze never moved from Mark's as he explained. "I've been in something like this before, when I was younger. Not with the cops, just me and a friend who wanted to help a guy we knew being threatened by drug-dealing scum. We set a trap for them, pretending we were buyers and we… well, we beat the crap outta them. All those years of having to defend myself in foster care and the institution paid off, I guess. I wasn't exactly a street fighter, but I knew some moves. I'd met Dave by that time and I called him when it was all over, and he took them in. This time Dave and a bunch of cops will be right there the whole time. If things get testy they'll step in."

"Just like that? This isn't a movie, Evan, where it's all

planned out, choreographed, rehearsed. Things could go really wrong. These are real criminals we're talking about."

"I know that," Evan said, more sharply than he had intended, and Mark stepped back from their embrace, his expression etched with worry. Evan immediately regretted his outburst. "Sorry..." He laid a light kiss on Mark's lips. "It'll be okay, sweetheart. I know this isn't a movie, but Dave won't go in without a solid plan. Castro and his men might be armed, but so will the cops—"

"That's supposed to make me feel better?" Mark groaned. "What if you get caught in the crossfire?"

"Mark, come on, babe. You are looking at this as the worst possible scenario. Chances are Castro will go for the deal, I'll back off and the police will take over."

"You make it sound so easy, and I just know it won't be." Mark put his arms around Evan again and laid his head on Evan's shoulder. "I won't sleep a wink if you agree to go through with Dave's plan."

"I've already decided."

Mark sighed. "I know you have. Damn you."

"I love you." Evan tilted Mark's head toward him and kissed his lips gently. "Very much."

Mark's eyes brimmed with tears as he stared at Evan. "I love you too, even though I hate you at this moment."

* * * *

Under Dave's supervision, Evan placed a call to Miguel Castro and told him he didn't have access to very much money, but that he had some cocaine in his possession he thought might be worth a lot of cash on the street.

"And how did you come by this cocaine, Mr. Ericson?" Castro asked, his voice deepening with suspicion.

"Kinda weird actually..." Evan began to spin the lie he and Dave had concocted together. "I was at this party up in Hollywood Hills, big house, lots of money there, lots of drugs being wheeled around. This guy kept coming on to me, promising me the earth for a night in his bed. I kept saying no and he got drunker and more insistent. I could tell he was in no condition to drive so I offered him a ride home—with no strings attached.

"He was so drunk he wasn't in any shape to do anything sexual anyway, so I felt okay about taking him home. He'd given me a card earlier with his home address on it, so I knew where to take him."

Castro sighed with obvious impatience, but Evan and Dave had decided he should ramble a bit until Castro told him to get to the point.

"Anyway, long story short, I got him into his house. I had to feel in his pockets for his keys, got 'em, opened the door, put him inside and left lickety-split. It wasn't until the next day I noticed he'd left his briefcase in the backseat of my car. I hadn't even known he had one when we left the party. So, anyway, I opened his case and found a large packet inside. I knew what it was soon as I saw it. I used to do drugs, y'see, but gave it up."

"Go on, Mr. Ericson," Castro rasped.

"Yeah, well, I figured there had to be at least over a pound of cocaine there. I mean, I don't really know what the street value would be, and frankly I was way too nervous about trying to sell it, so I've been sitting on it ever since. It doesn't go off, does it?" Evan, deliberately playing dumb, rolled his eyes at Dave.

"No, it doesn't. And this man you stole the cocaine from— he didn't try to find you and take it back?"

"No, he didn't. I kinda thought he would, and I'd have given it up easy, of course. But it's been six months now and no contact. Maybe I should just call him and tell him I have it. When you said 'stole from him' I felt bad."

"Yes, you could do that—on the other hand, you could give it to me and we will call your debt paid in full."

"That's tempting, I must admit," Evan said slowly as if thinking it over. "So, what d'you reckon it's worth?"

"Enough to cover your debt, that's all."

Evan glanced at Dave and grinned. The coke was worth a whole lot more than that, but of course Castro wasn't about to divulge the street price he could get for a pound of pure cocaine. Once it was 'cut' and sold for about four hundred dollars a gram, that one pound would be worth four times as much, maybe more.

"Okay, I guess I'll give it to you, but I want a receipt saying Dareck's debt is no longer mine."

Castro let out a sinister chuckle. Evan knew he considered him an idiot, but that was all right...all part of the plan.

"Of course," Castro continued, "I will have to verify that the cocaine is good. Be at seven hundred Forest Road in West Hollywood on Thursday at two p.m. I will send a man to check out your cocaine and if it is usable, we will have a deal."

"But I'm going to need some surety that the debt will be cleared."

"You will have that, if I am satisfied." The line went dead.

"Fucker," Evan muttered.

Dave didn't seem too happy. "We need him to be part of the sting, not just some lackey he's sending."

Evan thought for a moment or two. "How about if I only produce the sample, and say I'll give the rest when Castro approves it. I could also say I want to give it to him personally so I know it's in the right hands."

"That could work." Dave nodded in agreement. "And we'll be close by when you meet the man he sends Thursday."

Mark groaned. He'd been sitting in the corner listening to the conversation and Evan could tell he was not at all impressed. He looked angry.

"Evan..."

"I know you don't like this, sweetheart, but I'm committed now to seeing it through."

"Why? You don't owe LAPD anything. This is their business, not yours. I know Dave is a friend, but it seems to me he's asking too much of you."

Dave cleared his throat. "You're right, Mark, it's asking a lot, and I would never coerce Evan into doing this if he wasn't completely willing. I can only hope to assure you that we will do everything in our power to make sure this doesn't go wrong, and that Evan will be safe."

"I appreciate what you're saying, Dave, but I still think it's too dangerous. Why can't you have one of your guys take Evan's place? Impersonate him or something."

"Mark…" Evan rose from his seat and walked over to where Mark sat. He took the chair next to him and put an arm around his shoulders. "Castro has seen my picture, heard my voice — he'd never be fooled by someone impersonating me."

Mark sagged against him. "You're right, of course. I'll try to not worry. I'm such a liar. This whole thing is scaring me to death, but I know it's important to you. Even if it's for a reason I can't quite wrap my mind around, I respect it… and you."

"I'll make this up to you, I promise."

"You're darn right you will!"

* * * *

Evan opted not to say anything about the sting operation to Charles and Richard or any of the cast or crew. He was sure they would all try to talk him out of it, just like Mark had. It got a little awkward when Brett asked who the 'hunk' was he and Mark had been talking to as they'd walked to the exit with Dave after their last discussion.

"Uh, just an old friend of mine, Dave Franklin," Evan told him.

"Gay friend?"

Evan nodded. "He read in some paper I was shooting this movie and wanted to come say hi and good luck." He knew that story sounded flimsy, but it seemed Brett was too focused on the fact he considered Dave a hunk to give it a lot of thought.

"He is hot," Brett said. "Looks like ex-military. I love me a marine."

"You've had one?" Mark asked.

"No, I wish. Just a fantasy of mine. Is he single?"

"Uh, yeah, I think so." Evan realized he didn't actually know what Dave's status was these days. "I haven't seen him in a while and I didn't ask, sorry."

"Well, maybe next time you could introduce me. I might be too much of a twink for him, but I could show him a good time."

Evan grinned. "I think Dave might like that. If he's single, that is," he added hastily.

Richard joined them at that moment. "Brett, we need you again for your scene with Marsha. Charles wants to slightly change the dynamics between the two of you so I added some dialog for you. Okay?"

"Love it." Brett gave him a big smile. "Catch you guys later." He and Richard walked off together, Richard's hand on Brett's shoulder.

"He certainly charmed Charles and Richard," Evan remarked. "I wouldn't be surprised if Charles finds another vehicle for him."

"He's good, isn't he?" Mark said. "I hope his father doesn't get in the way of his career. I don't get the reason why he's so against Brett being an actor."

"Ron Lester has been in the business for a long time, Richard told me. Maybe he's seen stuff he doesn't want Brett caught up in."

Mark chuckled. "I think Brett could handle just about anything that comes his way. How come you didn't tell him Dave is a cop?"

"Well, that might have led to all kinds of questions, and I really don't want anyone here to know what's going on until it's over."

Mark grimaced. "Yeah, that."

"Let's go get some lunch," Evan said. "I only have one more scene and it's not scheduled till this afternoon."

"And I'm basically done until post-production, if they need me for reshoots. It's gonna feel strange not to come to the studio anymore."

Evan put an arm around Mark's waist and led him toward the exit. "I have a great idea."

"Oh yeah?"

"Once this mess with Castro is out of the way and we're done with the movie, what say you to the two of us taking a vacation? Somewhere nice, like the Mexican Riviera or Hawaii. We could lie on the beach all day, fuck all night. Sound good?"

Mark sighed. "Sounds like Heaven."

Evan pulled him closer. "Which part?"

"All of it."

Chapter Eleven

The dreaded day arrived and Mark was not about to let Evan go it alone.

"I won't be on my own, Mark," Evan said, sounding frustrated. "I'll have Dave and probably ten cops watching every move. And besides, it's just the preliminary meeting so the guy gets to see I have the real stuff. If he's happy I get to meet Castro later. It'll all be over before you can blink."

Earlier, he'd met with Dave and had been fitted with a wire so tiny it could've been a thread in the waistband of his briefs. The coke was put in the trunk of Evan's car and the small sample bag he'd stuffed in his jacket pocket.

"God…" Mark ran his fingers through his hair. "You make it all sound so damned easy. I appreciate you trying to calm me down, but I'd be a lot calmer if I can drive over there with you. I won't fuck it up by trying to go in with you. I'll wait outside. If any other thugs are watching, I'm just the boyfriend waiting for you. Nothing threatening in any of that, surely."

"Okay, if you promise to stay put in the car."

"I promise. I'll be peeing my pants while you're in there, but I'll sit tight."

Evan chuckled. "Please don't pee your pants. That upholstery is expensive." He pulled Mark into his arms. "It's going to be all right, Mark. After Castro is arrested we can go celebrate."

Mark breathed out a long, shuddering sigh and clung to Evan's hard body. "I'm gonna hold you to that, believe me."

Evan kissed him, a slow, all-consuming kiss that had Mark instantly hard. "Okay," Evan murmured against

Mark's lips, "time to go."

* * * *

Seven hundred Forest Avenue was the address of a coffee shop, The Brew. Evan walked inside, his hands in the pockets of his leather bomber jacket, one of which held the small sample of cocaine Dave had given him earlier. So far, it looked as if Evan's contact with Dave had gone unnoticed by Castro's men. He could only hope they were both correct in that assumption.

After a quick glance around the interior he focused on a young, dark-haired man who was staring at him. He made a slight gesture, pointing at the seat in front of him. This was either his contact or someone looking for a hook-up. He'd find out in a moment. The guy leaned forward in his seat as Evan sat down.

"You have it?"

"Why else would I be here?"

The man, who clearly needed a shave, frowned. "Follow me." He got up and headed to the back of the café, where a sign indicated the location of the restrooms. He opened a door next to the men's room and went in. Evan followed.

"Kinda cramped in here, isn't it?"

No answer, but Evan hadn't really expected one. The man scratched his unshaven chin then held out his hand and Evan placed the sample bag in his palm. It was quickly opened and tested. As Evan watched he had an almost overwhelming urge to shove the guy's face into the bag and beat the shit out of him. *Probably not a good idea…* But jerks like this really pissed him off.

After nodding, the man stuffed the bag into his pocket and opened the door. "Come with me." He led the way out of the café and approached Evan's car. "Get in."

"Wait a minute, I didn't agree to this."

"You want to see *Señor* Castro, yes? Get in the car."

Evan opened the passenger door. "Mark, get out," he

rasped. "Quickly." He gasped when he felt hard metal pressed into the small of his back.

"Your boyfriend comes too. Now get in, and no tricks or I shoot him."

Cursing under his breath, Evan walked around to the other side of the car. He didn't want to start looking around, but he hoped that Dave and his men were watching this change of plan. The thug got into the back seat and held his gun to Mark's head.

"No tricks, or I shoot."

"I heard you the first time," Evan said through clenched teeth. He put the car in gear and pulled away from the curb. "Where to?"

"First light, make a right. I'll tell you when to make the next turn."

A tense silence permeated the car's interior as they drove. Evan shot a quick glance at Mark. He was staring straight ahead, his normally expressive face devoid of emotion. *At least he's keeping calm right now...* He wanted to reach across the console and take his hand but thought better of it. Bristle-face might not approve. He didn't want to glance in the rearview mirror too often in case the jerk sitting behind them got the idea he might be checking for a car following them. He just hoped like hell Dave was somewhere close. And goddam it, but having Mark sitting next to him was something he just hadn't counted on. If this got ugly and Mark was hurt, he would never forgive himself. He should never have allowed him to come with him.

Should've told him flat out no! Would he have listened? Probably not, but oh, my God, if I'm responsible for him getting beaten up or worse – what the hell will I do?

"Take the next left, at the light."

Mark shifted and glanced at Evan. As if he had read Evan's mind, he stretched his hand out and rubbed Evan's thigh.

The fool behind them giggled and once again Evan wanted to lash out. He gripped the steering wheel until his knuckles turned white. He hoped he got to have at least one decent shot at the jerk's jaw.

"Over there, the green frontage. Pull in behind the building."

Now Evan did take a long look in the rearview mirror and his stomach dropped when he saw absolutely nothing behind them.

Shit… Three men wearing dark suits stood in a line facing them while Evan parked the car.

"Out."

Evan gave Mark an encouraging smile as they climbed out of the Audi. This did not look good at all. Had Dave figured Castro would bring an entourage along for the delivery? Trying to act as nonchalant as he could, he popped the trunk and retrieved the packet containing the cocaine. There was really nothing he could do but hand it over. He and Mark were fit, but four armed men made a formidable challenge, and for all he knew there might be more inside. The tiny wire hidden in the waistband of his briefs might be of use to the cops if he got into a conversation with Castro. All he could hope at this point was that he and Mark survived the next few minutes intact.

"So, where's the big boss?" He didn't address anyone in particular, just cast a stare around the group of thugs.

"Inside." One of them waved toward the only door he could see.

He and Mark walked toward it, coming to a halt when it was suddenly pushed open and a tall man dressed in an obviously expensive, light tan suit stepped out.

"Mr. Castro has been detained," he said in a cultured and unaccented voice. "I'll take that, and you can be on your way."

"Wait a minute." Evan knew he had to stall for time here, and also get an admission from one of these guys that it was Castro's deal. "I need some surety that the money Miguel Castro says I owe him is now settled with this cocaine. You guys are just taking it without any guarantee for me? I need to know that I'm in the clear, otherwise no deal."

The man in front of him chuckled. "You think you will walk away without handing it over? We didn't go to all this trouble for you to renege on the deal. Mr. Castro will be very unhappy with you...and your boyfriend. I don't advise that course of action."

Okay, so you've got Castro's name mentioned, several times already. Let it go so you and Mark can leave... Trying to ignore the trickle of nervous sweat that was coasting down his spine, he shrugged and made to hand over the packet of coke. "You got me. All you guys with guns are very convincing. Last time I dealt with a thug it was one-on-one."

Beside him, Mark coughed in warning, but the well-dressed man merely smirked.

"Hand it over, Mr. Ericson, and be on your way. And be glad I am not easily annoyed." He held out his hand and Evan gave him the packet.

Evan grabbed Mark by the arm and marched him back to the car. "Where the fuck is Dave and the backup? I can't believe they left us to those assholes' mercy. Jesus!"

They piled into the car and Evan, still fuming, backed it out of the parking area. As soon as he hit the street, three cars careened by them, heading for where Castro's men were entrenched. A large van screeched to a halt, effectively blocking the exit to the street.

"Holy shit!" Evan jammed on the brakes and leaped from the car.

"Evan!" Mark screamed at him then jumped out after him. "What the hell are you doing?" he yelled, clutching at his arm. Shots rang out and Mark pulled Evan up against the wall of the green building. "Don't you dare go anywhere near that. You hear me?"

Evan stared into Mark's blazing eyes and nodded. "Yeah, that was kinda dumb of me. Dave and his men probably waited till we were clear before charging in like that."

Silence fell, followed by the sound of someone moaning.

A few moments later several uniformed police officers led four of Castro's gang out and into the van. Dave showed up supporting the one who had taken the cocaine from Evan. Blood soaked the shoulder of his tailored suit.

Dave smirked. "Sam Horton, the lawyer…got in the way of a bullet."

"I need medical attention," Horton whimpered.

"You'll get it," Dave snapped. "And a lot more attention than you bargained for."

"Where's Castro?" Evan asked.

"Not here. We'll track him down soon as we get information from these goons." Dave assisted Horton into the back of one of the cars. "You did good, guys. We got all the conversation recorded, so we have something to pin on Castro at last."

"Let's go," Mark whispered in Evan's ear. "I need attention too."

Evan grinned. "You and me both."

* * * *

It took a couple of days before Mark felt the tension completely ease from his mind and body. Sometimes he couldn't quite believe that it was over and that they'd managed to pull it off. He'd been scared to death the entire time, and was always amazed when he reflected on the way Evan had retained such a cool demeanor, even though he knew his lover had been nervous, especially when Castro hadn't shown up to collect the coke. He knew he'd feel a lot more relaxed when they eventually put Castro behind bars, but Dave seemed pretty certain it was only a matter of time before they ran him down and arrested him.

Of course, a great deal of the tension easing was due to Evan, who had rushed him into bed as soon as they'd gotten back to his apartment. There had been some desperation in their lovemaking in the beginning. The adrenaline surge they'd both experienced from being in a dangerous situation had caused them to be slightly manic as they'd torn their clothes off, leaving a trail of shirts, shoes and jeans across the apartment floor before they'd crashed on top of the bed, tangled up in a knot of arms and legs. Bruising kisses had been exchanged and their hands had been less than gentle on each other's bodies. Mark had never felt so thoroughly fucked, and so happy to be so, as he had when Evan penetrated him and made him come hands-free from the erotic rush that had set every nerve ending in his body afire.

If he kept on thinking about that and the incredible bouts of sex they'd indulged in since then, he'd be walking around sporting a hard-on for the rest of his life. Which could be embarrassing, not to mention awkward.

The object of his desire walked out of the bedroom at that moment, shoving his cell phone into his pocket. "That was Richard. Charles has sent the film on to be edited, so I guess we're officially out of work again."

"Funny…" Mark chuckled. "It doesn't feel quite the same as when they fired me from the restaurant."

"They'll probably want us back for reshoots, so we can't go on our vacation yet." He flung himself down on the couch next to Mark and stretched out, his head in Mark's lap. "So, are you going to give your roomies notice that you're leaving and moving in with me?"

"If you still want me."

Evan snorted. "Silly boy." He turned and buried his face in Mark's crotch, worrying the already hard bulge with his lips through the denim.

"Gawd, Evan, you keep me in a constant state of arousal whenever you're around, and even when you're not."

"When am I not around? Remember I told you we're stuck like glue." He started to sing a fairly tuneless rendition of Sugarland's *Stuck Like Glue*.

Mark laughed. "Oh wow, I just found something you're not so good at…singing."

"Hey…" He looked up at Mark with wounded eyes then

laughed too. "Yep, nobody can kill a song quite like me."

Mark bent so he could kiss Evan. "But you're still perfect in every other way."

"Mmm...you know what saying stuff like that leads to, don'tcha?"

"Sex, and lots of it."

"Right." He sat up and pecked Mark's cheek. "Except not this time, darn it. We have to get ready for the *partay*. Richard said the other producers and their friends and spouses are gonna be there so we have to be social and kiss butts. Richard is so sure the movie is going to be a success he's already writing a sequel and wants to keep them interested."

"That would be fantastic. You and me in another movie. Hmm...presuming that Jeff and Peter continue their love affair."

Evan's eyes glinted wickedly. "That would be a condition of our working together. Detective and artist join forces as super sleuths. Like it?"

Mark grinned. "Love it."

* * * *

Mark kind of dreaded telling Perry and Andrew he was leaving, though he was sure they'd find another roommate soon enough. He hoped they didn't see it as a case of 'don't need you anymore', because that wasn't it at all. If he and Evan hadn't fallen in love, if they'd just been working actors together, he wouldn't have contemplated leaving the apartment he shared. It was comfortable enough and Andrew could be fun, and Perry... Well, Perry was Perry, and nothing much would ever change his tendency toward acerbic put-downs.

If ever anyone needed to get laid, it's Perry. He laughed to himself. When had he ever thought that sex was the answer to unhappiness? Not until Evan, obviously. And that meant good sex, very good sex.

"You're pretty quiet," Evan said, rubbing the back of his hand over Mark's thigh. They were driving to the wrap party in Evan's Audi. Mark had more or less given up driving his old clunker, leaving it in its parking space since he had moved in with Evan. At least now he could afford to trade it in and buy a new car.

"Just thinking 'bout things. How everything has changed for me, for the better. How lucky I am to have met you. Sometimes I think I'm gonna wake up and find it's all been a dream."

Evan chuckled. "That would be a pisser, wouldn't it? No movie, no me…and no you for me. Can't say I would like that at all, babe."

Mark leaned over and kissed Evan's neck. "I would hate it." He rested his head on Evan's shoulder and kept it there for the remainder of the drive. He'd almost drifted off to sleep when the car bumped over the entryway to the studio's parking lot.

Charles had apologized to everyone for having to throw the party here instead of his luxury apartment—the one Troy had trashed and which was still under repair. Richard had said he couldn't accommodate more than twenty guests at a time, so the studio had seemed a good option. The caterers had done a beautiful job, Mark noted as he and Evan walked in. Several round tables were scattered about, each one with its own colored overhead lighting courtesy of the lighting engineers. A bar stood in one corner and a long buffet table in another. Already the studio was fairly crowded.

"Wow, more people that I expected to see," Evan remarked. He straightened his suit jacket then took Mark's hand and approached a group where Charles and Richard were holding court. "I'm not too good at this," he whispered, "so you'll have to do all the talking."

Mark laughed. "You jest, of course. You are the one with the personality of ten men and the charisma to go with it."

"You think so?" Evan's eyes twinkled at him under the

lights.

"*You* know so, you faker."

Charles turned and beckoned them forward, a big smile on his face. "Ah, here they are…" A round of introductions began and Mark's head swam from the number of names he knew he'd never remember. He breathed a sigh of relief when Marsha, with Brett in tow, joined them.

"Marsha, you look stunning," Evan told her, and she did. Her blonde hair was coiffed to perfection and she wore a black gown that sparkled with some kind of stone Mark couldn't begin to figure out. She looked the epitome of elegance.

"Not bad for an old broad, huh?" She giggled and swung a black beaded purse in front of them. "I've got a mirror and a ton of makeup in here for emergencies."

"Not that you'll need any of that," Mark said. Marsha had come a long way from the rather stiff-smiled woman they'd first met all those weeks ago.

"Flatterer." Marsha laughed gaily and put an arm around Brett's waist. "And I have my own charming gay man to fetch me drinks all night."

Brett leaned in and kissed her on the cheek. "And before I get blitzed and can't form coherent sentences," she continued, "I just want to say it has indeed been a pleasure working with all of you. Evan, I was dubious at first when Richard told me what you'd done prior to this, but if the critics don't give you kudos for your performance in this movie, their heads are all up their asses!"

"Thank you, Marsha." Evan took her hand and kissed it. "That means a lot to me, especially coming from someone as experienced as you."

"Hey, I've seen some of the rushes, kid, and you shine… really *shine*." Marsha turned to Mark. "And you're not so bad either. You make a great couple. Richard told me he's writing a sequel. I called him a shithead for killing me off in this one!"

* * * *

The party proceeded with everyone seemingly having a good time. Mark and Evan were constantly surrounded by people they'd never seen before in their lives, but as Evan had mentioned earlier, they had to smile and kiss butts. Mark's jaw ached from the smile he had permanently plastered on his face.

"Wish we had some of our own friends here," he muttered to Evan at one point. "Apart from the cast and crew, there's no one we know."

"We'll have our own party at my place — at *our* place — to celebrate you moving in, and finishing the movie." Evan ran his hand up and down Mark's back. "Can't wait to get you home."

"Home…that sounds nice."

Evan turned to him, but whatever he was about to say was interrupted when the studio door crashed open and a man holding a gun strode in. Mark's first thought was that maybe he could be a lone wolf terrorist. The man had a dark complexion. He appeared wild-eyed and haggard, and his clothes, which might have been impressive at one time, hung raggedly from his shoulders, the jacket ripped and covered in dirt. A heavy silence fell over the assembled crowd.

"Who the hell are you?" Charles demanded. "Leave, before we call the police."

"The police?" The intruder sniggered. "The police will not save the one I have come to kill."

"Are you mad?"

"Yes, I am mad… Mad enough to shoot the one who ruined me, who thought he was so clever that he could take me down. Perhaps he has succeeded, but he will not live to enjoy his success. Evan Ericson," he hissed, "show yourself, or I start shooting everyone in here."

"There is no one here by that name," Charles said.

"Liar!" He raised the gun and aimed it at Charles' chest.

"You will be the first—"

"Stop." To Mark's horror, Eric stepped forward to face the man. "I'm Evan Ericson." *No, no, no!*

"You've ruined me, you fucking little faggot! The cops are right behind me, but before they get me, I am going to kill you. Your death will at least give me some pleasure in jail, when I remember your dead body lying on this floor in a pool of your own blood."

Mark heard a siren somewhere outside, but he knew the cops would be too late. Castro, for it surely had to be him, was going to kill Evan, and he couldn't allow that. He was just about to leap forward and push Evan out of the way when a shot rang out and Castro screamed. He fell to the ground clutching his leg, his gun falling from his grasp. Before he could reach for it, Evan was on him, his foot trapping Castro's wrist, pinning it to the floor.

Castro let fly a stream of curses, mostly unintelligible, as he struggled to free himself. Evan yanked the drug dealer to his feet then laid him out with one powerful uppercut to his chin.

Evan turned and grinned. "Thanks, Marsha."

It was then that Mark saw Marsha standing alongside an open-mouthed Brett, holding a small pistol in her hand, her beaded bag open. "Never go anywhere without this puppy these days," she said, smiling at the gaping crowd. "A girl can't be too safe, now can she?"

A cheer went up amid applause and laughter, then the door once again was thrown open and Dave, heading a phalanx of officers, guns drawn, strode into the studio.

Evan pointed at Castro, who was still out cold. "Thanks to Marsha Simmons, star of *Burning Hearts*, we're all safe and sound, and there's the scumbag you want."

* * * *

After Castro had been carried out and the officers had finished gathering statements from the witnesses to his attempted assault, the party started to disassemble.

"A night to remember," Charles said, giving Evan a hug. "I don't think Richard has to look too far for the plot of his next movie. It's been given to him on a plate."

Richard chuckled. "Not to mention the free publicity we garnered. This will be big news tomorrow. I'll make sure of it."

As pleased as Mark was to hear all this, he couldn't wait for the moment when he and Evan would be on their own. This night had proven to him, though in reality he'd never had any doubts, just how much he loved Evan. In that fleeting moment of terror when he'd envisioned Evan being shot by that lunatic, his whole future, bleak and empty without the man he loved, had flashed before his eyes. He didn't realize how violently he had been shaking until Evan had taken him in his arms and had held him till the tremors had passed.

"Can we go home now?" he whispered in Evan's ear and Evan nodded. They said their goodnights to anyone still there then stepped outside, the cool late-evening breeze a welcome balm on Mark's face. Evan slipped off his jacket and breathed a long sigh of relief. Mark followed suit, draping his jacket over his shoulder.

"Man, this has been a night I don't want a repeat of anytime soon." He slid an arm around Mark's waist and pulled him in close. "You all right, babe?"

"Now I am, but it'll take me a while to get over how close you came to getting killed."

"Yeah, there's nothing quite like the reality check of having a gun pointed at you by a freaking maniac." He smiled grimly. "Who knew Marsha would be a gun-totin' mama?"

They managed to laugh, even if it was a little forced. "Fancy walking for a while? I like the feel of the cool air after all that trauma."

Mark nodded. "Sounds good."

They strolled hand in hand down the long boulevard,

which was mostly deserted, save for a car cruising by now and then.

"We should pick a date for our party," Evan said suddenly. "I was thinking next weekend, Friday or Saturday. What d'you think?"

"Uh-huh…"

Evan squeezed his hand. "You okay?"

"I'm still a bit shaken up, I guess."

Evan guided him into a walled garden area they were passing. He led Mark deep into the shadows cast by enormous eucalyptus and pine trees, then took him into his arms and kissed him, long and slow, his tongue moving over Mark's with a tender urgency. Mark moaned. Their kiss was sweet, but the underlying passion was unmistakable.

"Evan…"

"Shh, shh…"

They sank onto the ground under one of the trees and Evan used his jacket to cushion Mark's head.

"You think this is okay?" Mark whispered. "There might be homeless people sleeping in here."

"Don't think they'll care. I just want to hold you, kiss you, feel you grow hard against me. Take your mind off what happened earlier."

"I'm already hard."

Evan chuckled and palmed the bulge in Mark's pants. He pulled down Mark's zipper and fondled the hard shaft he found there. He eased the hot and heavy flesh out from its cotton confines then leaned down so he could lick at the leaking head. A frisson of exquisite pleasure surged through Mark's body.

"Mmm," Evan murmured, "nobody ever tasted as good as you."

Mark whimpered and bucked his hips upward, giving Evan more of his cock. Evan slid his lips up and down the hard flesh at the same time as he pumped it rapidly. Every nerve ending in Mark blazed with desire. He didn't care where they were, in some small public park in Burbank, or that what they were doing was open to the eyes of anyone who might happen by. All he could sense and feel and smell was the wonderful man he was with, whose clever tongue and lips were giving him a blow job like no other—one to remember always. He ran his fingers through Evan's soft, shaggy hair, clutching at the silky strands as his orgasm roiled in his balls.

"Evan, Evan, Evan…" He groaned out his lover's name over and over as his body was consumed in heat, and he exploded into Evan's mouth, shaken to his core by the force of his climax. Evan milked him to the last drop, kissing and tonguing the slit until there was no more for him. He opened Mark's shirt and dragged his mouth up over Mark's bare, warm torso, nuzzling, nibbling and driving Mark slightly out of his mind. When he reached Mark's lips he paused, his silver-gray eyes so close they were visible even in the darkness that surrounded them.

"I love you, Mark Henderson," he murmured. "I think I have from the moment I first kissed you—and I will, until the day I die."

Mark moaned and pressed his lips to Evan's, letting the scent and taste of his own cum fill his senses along with the sweet, moist warmth of Evan's breath.

"I love you too," Mark whispered when at last they broke free of their kiss. "I love you so much, that tonight I didn't know how I could have gone on without you if you'd died."

"Then I promise I won't die." Evan smiled and rubbed their noses together.

"I have to take care of you now," Mark said, tugging at Evan's zipper.

"Uh, you're a little late." Evan chuckled, stilling Mark's hand. "I came same time as you—and oh boy—but it's gross down there. All cold and sticky and stuff."

They laughed helplessly as they stood and gathered their jackets from the ground.

"Sorry," Mark said, "I don't have any Kleenex on me."

"There's some in the car, but by the time we get back there

it won't matter. A nice hot shower awaits me…and you."

"And you know what happens when we share a shower."

"Exactly. Sex, and lots of it!"

Epilogue

Six months later

"That'll do it for today, guys." Fashion photographer Joel Styles gave them both thumbs up while his staff began to disassemble his equipment. "This is gonna be one of the best spreads I've done in a long time. You two are so freakin' photogenic."

Evan and Mark voiced their thanks as they slipped into their robes. They had just completed yet another fashion shoot, this one for a leading men's underwear spread in *Vanity Fair*.

"I'll never understand why that modeling agency you worked for let you go, Evan," Joel remarked.

"That's what I kept saying when we first met," Mark said in agreement.

"I bet they're grinding their teeth now." Joel grinned. "They couldn't have paid for better publicity than you both got for free." He hugged them one at a time. "See you at the *VF* party tomorrow night?"

"Yes, we'll be there," Evan told him. "See you tomorrow."

They waved Joel goodbye. "Let's get dressed and grab something to eat on the way home," Evan said. "I am *starving*."

"Me too, but don't eat too much. We're meeting Kyle and Josh for dinner later." They entered the small dressing room Joel's studio provided. "Who knew by just standing around having your picture taken you could work up such an appetite?"

Evan waited until Mark threw aside his robe then stuck

a finger in the elastic waistband of the red briefs Mark had been modeling and snapped it over his butt. "To say nothing of the appetite you work up in me when you're only wearing skivvies."

"Ow." Mark grinned at his lover. "Glad I still interest you."

"Are you kidding? There's enough interest to last at least sixty years."

"Sweet." Mark leaned in to kiss Evan before they started dressing.

Their lives had changed radically in the last six months. Miguel Castro's attempt to kill Evan had grabbed headlines in both newspapers and television. Castro's subsequent trial and sentence to twenty years in jail had fueled the gossip columns, calling Evan a hero and Marsha Simmons one cool lady. The publicity had been great for all of them, hyping *Burning Hearts* to almost Oscar-nomination status and a place in the Cannes Film Festival, even before its general release date had been announced. Those who claimed to have seen the movie in private showings declared it a winner, and its cast major stars of the future.

Evan and Mark could only hope that part was a solid prediction, although they were both sensible and grounded enough to know the winds of good fortune in the entertainment business could shift rapidly and without warning. Still, their newfound fame was heady to say the least. Together they had appeared on several morning shows and late-night shows, and there had been offers of new films to keep them busy reading scripts.

Even the often scurrilous columns in the sleazy tabloids reporting about the year Evan had spent in the porn industry hadn't slowed their steady rise through the A list. It amazed Evan how many people he'd never met or spoken to during that time remembered so many little things he'd said and done.

"Look at this." He'd shown Mark one of the articles when they'd been standing in line at their local grocery store. "I remember one day, Dean—that was Evan Ericson's porn name—couldn't get it up so I offered to be his 'fluffer'— that's porn jargon for someone who'll help get you ready— and he was only too happy to accept." Evan had laughed. "As if!"

The woman standing in front of them in line, along with the cashier, had enjoyed Evan's reading the article out loud and asked for their autographs, while Mark did his usual blushing routine.

For Mark, this change in his life didn't make him happy just because he had a brand-new car—a bright red Jaguar F-type convertible—or a wardrobe of new clothes, or the fact he didn't have to skimp on meals anymore. His true happiness came from the fact that as the weeks and months had gone by, he had fallen more and more in love with Evan, and if the affection his lover constantly showed him was any indication, the feeling was entirely mutual.

At the end of their busy days, if they had a free evening, there was nothing they both enjoyed more than to share a glass of wine, curl up on the sofa in each other's arms and watch a movie. Either that or have mind-melting sex in ways that were becoming more and more inventive as they gained more and more knowledge of each other's bodies, their likes and dislikes—Mark couldn't think of any of the latter—and the hidden, secret places that when kissed or caressed turned them into each other's willing sex slaves.

As they left Joel's studio Evan said, "Why don't we just order in a pizza and have them come over?" He was referring to their dinner date with Kyle and Josh.

"Not a bad idea. Kyle loves pizza. Not so sure about Josh."

"Call and ask. We could pick up a salad on the way home."

"Okay." Mark was a little surprised that Kyle and Josh were still an item. They seemed so mismatched to Mark. Kyle with his pixie-like demeanor and off-the-wall sense of humor, and Josh, so serious and not a great source of conversation.

"He's very deep," Kyle had told Mark. "A thinker, not an

action man."

"Hmm, what does that do for you in bed if he's just thinking about it?" Mark's snarky comment had made Kyle roar.

"Oh, don't worry 'bout that. In bed he's all action."

So, that was good. Mark grinned, recalling the conversation. He punched in Kyle's speed number on his cell and left him a message regarding the pizza.

He was glad they'd managed to keep in touch with all their friends despite their hectic schedules. Perry and Andrew had taken his leaving the apartment he shared with them philosophically, and hadn't had any trouble finding a new roommate, another actor looking for work. They managed to get together for drinks occasionally, and Evan had arranged for Dave and Brett to finally meet. It seemed theirs was a romance in progress.

Richard had called Evan the week before to tell them his script for his new movie venture was ready and he wanted them to read it. They would be reprising their former roles as artist and detective in a ripped-from-the-headlines case — in actuality their own headline case involving Miguel Castro.

"Couldn't have asked for a better detective story," Richard had told them, "and it fits real well with the fifties setting. Charles said he'll direct and, oh yeah, I've written a scene for quick-draw Marsha."

"I was just thinking about that new script of Richard's," Mark said as they climbed into his Jag. "D'you think we'll have another nude love scene?"

"Sweetheart…" Evan shifted in his seat so he could pull Mark into an embrace. "That is a must. It'll be written into our contract. After all…" He teased Mark's lips with the tip of his tongue, "we can't let all that practice go to waste, now can we?"

"Absolutely not," Mark mumbled.

He opened to Evan, and as their kiss deepened and went on and on, he thought through the daze that Evan's kisses always wrapped around his brain, *And there's no time like the present for a whole lot more practice.*

All I'll Ever Need

Excerpt

Chapter One

Edward Conway couldn't remember just how long he'd been standing on the opposite side of the street from the Rockin' Bar's entrance, but he was sure of one thing—his feet, hands and nose were way too cold, and if he didn't grow a pair and get his ass inside, he'd most likely come down with some kind of flu-related ailment. It was an unseasonably chilly night in southern California, one he'd been unprepared for, venturing out earlier without his bomber jacket that would have shielded him from the bitter wind.

"God, but you're a pussy," he muttered. What could be so terrible? It was a gay bar—a place he'd wanted to visit ever since he'd arrived in LA, just to see what it was like. Maybe he'd meet someone nice, talk, share a kiss perhaps… Then who knows? There was always a chance it might lead to something more, something he'd been aching for, for a long time, things he so acutely knew were missing from his life. Warmth, companionship, a friend he could open up to, a chance to feel needed... Maybe even loved.

"Go on then..." He took a tentative step forward onto the concrete strip that separated him from what he so desperately wanted. The cracked surface of the narrow one-way street now seemed as wide as the Grand Canyon, and just as formidable to cross. But cross it he must, and when he reached the other side he'd simply push his way through the door and join the throng of people inside. What could be so difficult about that?

Edward had been in Los Angeles for only four weeks, but his hometown of Ellingsworth, North Carolina, already seemed a distant place, both in miles and in his memories. He'd wanted to get out of Ellingsworth so badly he could almost taste the freedom it would bring him. When he'd finally cut himself loose from his so-called friends and family, it had been with such little regret that he still marveled at how easy it had been in the end.

After finally making the supreme effort to cross the street, he stood staring at the door of the Rockin' Bar, closed against the chill of the night air. All he had to do was push it open and he could enter into the warmth he was sure awaited him on the other side. The decision was taken out of his hands when two young guys brushed past him, swung the door open, and one of them, giving Edward a sweet smile, held it for him.

"Th-thanks..." He grabbed the handle then followed them inside. Edward had only ever been in one gay bar before, and that had been in Charlotte, North Carolina, a city as different from Los Angeles as beer is from champagne. Edward couldn't quite believe just how big a space the bar encompassed — it was at least half a football field long — and there was an upper floor — and everywhere there were people — mostly men, standing practically shoulder to shoulder or dancing on the huge wooden floor in the center of the bar. The noise was incredible. A wall of sound surrounded him. Laughter, chatter and the thump, thumping bass he'd only been vaguely aware of outside on the street now overwhelmed his senses, made him feel vibrant… Alive.

He headed for the bar where the bartender, a hottie wearing shorts and a big smile, asked him, "What'll it be, handsome?"

"You have Stella?"

"On tap, just for you, my pretty. Small or large?"

"Maybe a small one, to start." The bartender's sunny smile and flirty attitude went a long way to make Edward relax and feel glad he'd made the decision to get out and test the waters of LA's gay scene.

"On the house." The bartender placed a glass of amber liquid in front of Edward. "Name's Gary by the way."

"Edward — and thanks for the beer."

They shook hands across the bar. "Pleasure. Like to look after our first timers, so you'll come back."

Edward had no doubt he'd come back. When Gary left to take care of his other customers, Edward took a long swig of his Stella, savoring the refreshing coolness and slightly nutty taste. He glanced around the bar, avoiding too much eye contact with the other patrons, but taking in the general mix of guys his own age and some older men talking, smiling, laughing in groups or couples, or simply standing alone, like himself. Despite the volume of music there was a mellow ambience present in the bar, and even the need to shout to be heard wasn't overly irritating. He couldn't help but compare these people with the grim faces he'd left behind.

After months of muttered innuendo directed his way in the workplace, unreturned phone calls from those he'd once considered friends, silence and hard stares from his parents, bullying taunts and punches from his brother, he'd had enough. The job he'd applied for on the Internet had seemed at first to be a bit of a stretch for him. It had meant relocation, new surroundings, no one he knew nearby — daunting prospects without a doubt — but wasn't that exactly what he'd wanted? To shake himself free of the depression that had dogged him night and day, the inner loneliness he had felt sure would consume him completely and lead him to do something really stupid, like end his life, all because he was seen to be different in the eyes of those around him.

But was he really so different? Hadn't he seen on the TV masses of people like him celebrating the overturning of Proposition 8 in California, the legalization of same-sex marriage in sixteen states, the end of DOMA and DADT? The world was changing, and Edward wanted to be a part of that change, wanted recognition for himself, what he was, who he was. More than anything he wanted to find another like himself, someone who would understand him, love him unconditionally just as he would love in return.

Well, that wasn't going to happen in Ellingsworth, North Carolina — a too-small town where everyone knew not only your name but everything else about you, too. Where it was considered only right to correct what they perceived to be wrong, no matter who it hurt, no matter the fallout. When Edward, buoyed by the progress he could see all around the country, had come out to his family, he truly had not expected the hateful reaction he'd received.

They hadn't thrown him out, but it might have been better if they had. His father had told him to never mention such a hideous thing again, never to tell anyone else of his perversion, and to pray nightly to God for deliverance from his sinful ways. However, his brother, Craig, wasn't satisfied with his family's judgment. He'd made it his business to let everyone they knew in on Edward's confession. Even his father's wrath couldn't shut Craig up, and before long Edward had found himself ostracized by just about everyone he came in contact with. The world might be changing, but not Edward's world, not in Ellingsworth, North Carolina. His decision to leave had been met with indifference both at home and where he worked at the local bank. He'd had a feeling the manager was getting ready to fire him anyway, after being informed of Edward's unnatural tendencies. Yes, brother Craig had done an excellent job of character assassination.

Thanks, bro, hope I never have to look at your acne-ridden face again…

More books from Pride Publishing

Book one in the Dangerous Dancers series

A reporter and the thief he's investigating both fall for a golden dancer, forging a ménage of love and lies that could send one to prison and one to the morgue.

Book one in the Anthem trilogy

An ocean of possibility. For love, revenge and murder.

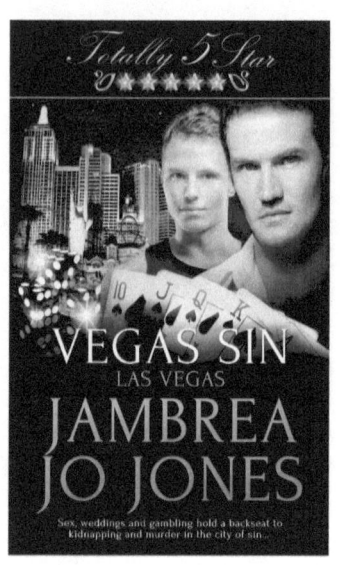

Part of the Totally 5 Star collection

Sex, weddings and gambling hold a back seat to kidnapping and murder in the city of sin…

Andrew had no intention of ever going back home. But circumstances force him to face his painful past and the friend who betrayed him.

About the Author

J.P. Bowie

J.P Bowie was born in Scotland and toured British theatres in numerous musical shows including Stephen Sondheim's Company.

Emigrated to the States and worked in Las Vegas, Nevada for the magicians Siegfried and Roy as their Head of Wardrobe at the Mirage Hotel. Currently living in Henderson, Nevada.

J.P. Bowie loves to hear from readers. You can find contact information, website details and an author profile page at https://www.pride-publishing.com/